PLEASURE BOUND

Also by Alison Tyler

A Is for Amour
Afternoon Delight
B Is for Bondage
Best Bondage Erotica
Best Bondage Erotica, Volume 2
C Is for Coeds
Caught Looking (with Rachel Kramer Bussel)
D Is for Dress-Up
E Is for Exotic
Exposed
F Is for Fetish
Frenzy
G Is for Games
Got a Minute?
H Is for Hardcore
Hide and Seek (with Rachel Kramer Bussel)
Hurts So Good
The Happy Birthday Book of Erotica
Heat Wave
I Is for Indecent
J Is for Jealousy
K Is for Kinky
L Is for Leather
Love at First Sting
Luscious
The Merry Xxxmas Book of Erotica
Naughty or Nice?
Never Have the Same Sex Twice
Open for Business
Playing with Fire
Red Hot Erotica
Slave to Love
Three-way

PLEASURE BOUND

TRUE BONDAGE STORIES

EDITED BY
ALISON TYLER

CLEIS
PRESS

Published in the United States by Cleis Press Inc., P.O. Box 14697, San Francisco, California 94114.

Printed in Canada.
Cover design: Scott Idleman
Cover photograph: © pbnj productions/Brand X/Corbis
Text design: Frank Wiedemann
Cleis Press logo art: Juana Alicia
First Edition.
10 9 8 7 6 5 4 3 2 1

ISBN 13: 978-1-57344-354-8

"Before Sleep Does" by Sommer Marsden originally appeared in *Never Have the Same Sex Twice* (Cleis Press, 2008).

For SAM,
always

Why comes temptation, but for man to meet and master and crouch beneath his foot, and so be pedestaled in triumph?

—Robert Browning

The strongest is never strong enough to be always the master, unless he transforms strength into right, and obedience into duty.

—Jean-Jacques Rousseau

Contents

INTRODUCTION: ARE YOU READY TO BE CAPTURED?

Are you sure?

You might think you're primed and set—but hold up a second. Let me share something with you. Allow me to give you an insight into my world. See, every so often I find myself in a tight spot. Work becomes all consuming, and I have a difficult time pulling back, being the clearheaded Editrix who moves a comma, caps a word, cuts a bit of redundancy.

Instead, I wind up staring at the computer screen, as bound in place as the lovers in the story, held tight with steel or leather, with cuffs or silk ties, with rope or with words alone. I'll sit for minutes after reading a whole story without realizing the tale has ended. Even my breathing will slow, and I'll stay at my desk as frozen as if I've been put there by a master of my own, as if I've been given the instructions to sit.

To stay.

To wait.

And then, when I'm done—all right, you know me. I'm *never* really done—but when night falls and I manage to break away, close the file, shut the PowerBook, I am dizzy with want; hungry beyond measure; trapped in that jittery *Fuck me, take me* place that only a good, strong hand on my wrist can calm; only a low, dangerous throb of a command can still.

Talk about bringing your work home with you.

This has happened to me with every last one of the forty-seven anthologies I've edited.

But *Pleasure Bound* proved even more consuming than my usual collections. Why? Because these stories are based on true tales. Think about that for a moment. Yes, some names have been changed, and characteristics have been added or deleted for legal reasons. But trust me, there are no innocents here to protect.

So while, as always, I lost myself in the stories, this time I experienced an added thrill, knowing that somewhere—maybe long ago, maybe just last weekend—these scenarios unfolded in real life, in real time.

How could you read a line like, *"I'm going to hurt you, Tess"*—and not hear *his* voice, low and dark, right next to your ear? Sure, those words might have jarred you in a standard fictional sex tale, but I promise this—they will downright shake you to your core when you gaze up at the name of the writer at the top of the page. Seeing that Tess Danesi wrote this piece, and knowing that this situation happened to her, takes the level up a notch or ninety-nine.

Be prepared to be moved. Be prepared to be stunned.

How should you get ready?

Here's my advice: Keep your back straight. Don't speak unless you're spoken to. Don't forget to breathe as you turn the page. And don't forget that someone you know (maybe the woman in the cubicle right next to yours, maybe the man standing at your side in the elevator) lived through every single scene in this book.

Do you have your safeword close at hand?

Are you ready to be *Pleasure Bound*?

XXX,
Alison Tyler

HANDFAST

Nikki Magennis

for C

Of all the ties, ropes, tape, cuffs, ribbons, and restraints that have held me down, up, and spread-eagled, there's one kind of bond that will never come loose.

Your hands, and the sweet insistence in your fingertips, my dear. The certainty of how you arrange things. The way you know me—which way I turn and how far.

How your mouth can anchor me, even without words. How I am trapped by your smile.

One touch, I am undone and most of all long to be fixed by a kiss.

Hold on, sweetheart—hold on tight. Don't let go.

THE VISIT

A. D. R. Forte

I took the bus to see him, headed north on a cloudy morning from the gravel parking lot of the station, through Texarkana and Little Rock and Nashville and all the nameless places in between; wearing the old sweatshirt he'd given me once, hands tucked deep in the pockets against the cold. I could have flown there, upgraded to first class with my platinum something or the other. I could have worn heels and lipstick and my charcoal wool suit, the one that makes me look taller and older and pretty damned hard to ignore.

But I didn't. I wanted to curl up on the grubby bus seat with my feet propped on my backpack and my headphones in, just another face on the bus.

I wanted to watch the world outside go by, the strangers in the seat next to me come and go: The middle-aged Mexican guy in the cowboy hat who didn't speak a word of English. The cute girl with chipped nail polish and bright red hair who talked to me about movies and asshole exes, and a whole lot more that

I don't remember because at some point I was thinking about fucking her. Nobody at all from somewhere in Illinois to Chicago so that I took my sneakers off and lay down across both seats, and thought about seeing him after so long.

What would it be like? Email and phone calls weren't the same as being there. Friendship wasn't the same as what we'd been before, whatever that had been.

I wanted the late-night stops at gas stations and deserted bus stations in insignificant towns where I listened to other passengers' conversations and made up the rest of their lives once we got back on the road—finishing in my head the stories that I'd never hear the end of.

I wanted soda pop and a greasy hot dog at the downtown bus station in Chicago while I waited for my transfer and watched it rain.

When I made it to him, I wanted to feel like myself again, having shed the shiny satiny veneer I'd somehow picked up somewhere along the line, the shell of sensible decisions and safe bets and all the stuff I'd sold out for. I wanted to feel vulnerable and impossible again. I wanted to be uncluttered again.

Especially with him. I had to be.

When I left the bus for the last time sometime after ten P.M. at the final station for me, I didn't call him to say I'd arrived. I took out a paperback and sat on my backpack on the floor, ignoring the empty rows of linked plastic seats that had no doubt been installed twenty years before and probably hadn't been all that comfortable back then either. I looked up only when I saw a pair of jeans over the edge of my book and heard the jingle of keys.

He stood there, thumbs hooked in his pockets, looking like time hadn't happened to him; like all the years between the last time I'd seen him and that moment didn't exist.

I was the fraud. I was the one who'd gone and changed.

But then he reached out a hand to help me up, and I put my book down. I stood, and he cupped the nape of my neck, pulled my head toward him. It wasn't a gentle gesture. It wasn't a gesture that allowed me to resist.

Beneath the mint of his gum, I tasted coffee and cigarettes, and I closed my eyes, forgetting time as he forced his tongue into my mouth. I felt my nipples harden and my heart pound with conditioned fear because it knew what came after his kiss. It remembered this touch, this male scent, this body pressing against mine.

Nothing had changed for us. I had been stupid to think it would.

He told me he had to go back to work. Someone was hanging out for him but he had to close up at the bowling alley. I nodded and picked up my backpack, licking my lower lip that hurt, bruised now. But I deserved it.

A few years before, at some point when I'd been so full of my success I couldn't see past my nose, I'd asked why he insisted on such shitty jobs, why he was so stubborn about it.

He'd laughed at me, and even over the phone I could tell he'd been genuinely amused by my tirade.

"You sound really fucking self-righteous right now," he'd told me. And I'd bitten my tongue in shame.

"It's okay," he'd said, reading the guilt in my silence as if he could see my face. "You'll still be my sweet, brilliant little cunt no matter how full of yourself you get. No matter what."

He'd said it lovingly and cruelly, and I'd known he meant it. I knew that if I ever saw him again, I would have to pay for saying it. And I'd sat there holding the phone and ached for him, just like I'd ached for him from the very start.

Like I still ache for him, even now.

He's the only one I've ever needed that way.

That night, I followed him out of the bus station and to his car. We drove through the city and I leaned back in the passenger seat, looked out at skyscrapers and sidewalks with that sense of excitement I always get from being in a place I've never been before. At a stoplight I turned to look at him, and realized I was leaning toward him, like I always used to. He smiled and ran a finger down my nose, tapped the end of it.

"I'm glad to see you again," he told me.

And I couldn't find anything to say, so I didn't answer.

The bowling alley was already closed, and the other guy left almost as soon as we got there, leaving us alone.

"I won't be too long," he told me. "Sit still until I get back."

I did, perched on a stool behind the counter with rows and rows of grubby shoes smelling of Lysol behind me, and rows of darkened lanes ahead. The alley wasn't new, wasn't a franchise, not the kind of place I ever went to anymore. But it was the kind of place where he and I had spent Friday nights once upon a time.

I wondered if I shouldn't have come, if the visit had been a bad idea. I second-guessed myself even as I ran my tongue over my bruised lip again, afraid the kiss in the station lobby had been just my own wishful thinking. That this would only end in disappointment.

"Good girl," he said, when he came back to find me still in place, but fidgeting with boredom and anxiousness.

"Come here."

And without thinking, I rose and followed him, doubt forgotten when he ordered me.

He asked if I'd ever seen how a bowling alley worked and I

told him no, so he showed me the machine area behind the lanes, the huge gears and the rows of silent pins. Then he took me to the control room off to the side. Levers ranged down one wall and shelves and clipboards the other. The walls were painted turquoise blue, faded and grimy with years of grease and dust, rendered even more dingy by fluorescent light from the dirty bulbs overheard. The smell of oil and metal lingered in the air.

"How would you like to be fucked here?"

I was exhausted and felt filthy from traveling for more than a day. My back ached and my eyes hurt, and I hadn't eaten except for the lone hot dog in Chicago and countless bottles of caffeinated soda.

I looked at him and my breath caught in my throat.

"Yes," I said.

"Yes what?" he asked as he came to stand before me, and I took a deep breath. It scared me that it came so easily, that we'd picked up our old ways so seamlessly.

"Yes, Sir." And I was trembling as I said it. "Please."

He yanked my sweatshirt off and the T-shirt under that. He smiled to find me without a bra and shook his head.

"What a slut. Still."

I swallowed and shook my head.

"No," I said.

"No?" he replied, eyebrows raised, hands on his hips.

I tightened my stomach. I was breathing too shallowly, but I needed too much. I could barely think.

I tilted my chin up and swallowed.

"No. I'm not a slut," I said.

He grabbed my shoulder and spun me around, pushed me toward the wall beside the door. Instinctively I put my hands out, one clutching the door frame, the other pressed to the wall. I felt his breath hot on my neck as he leaned into me, his weight forcing me against the wall. His hands squeezed my breasts, kneaded them so that they rubbed against the rough surface.

I squeezed my eyes shut, disgusted at my own sweaty dirtiness, disgusted even more at the thought of my bare skin on the grimy wall, frustrated at the relentless pleasure filling my clit as my ever-sensitive nipples responded to cold and pain and pressure and shame. I could feel his cock, rock hard, pressed into my ass through my jeans and his.

His lips brushed my neck, kissing softly: gentle breaths and tiny, wet touches of his tongue with each kiss. I writhed, trying to get away from the tickling sensation that made my clit pulse with need; trying to get away from his hands that brutalized my tits, fingers pinching my nipples so hard I screamed from pain. I heard my nails scrape painfully on the metal of the door frame. My heartbeat was choking me. God, oh, god. How did he manage to do this?

The punishment left my breasts suddenly and I gasped, sobbed for breath.

"I like this haircut on you," he said, lips still at the base of my neck. "Your hair isn't in the way."

I laughed, laughter tinged with hysteria.

"Great. Thanks." My voice cracked on the 'Thanks.'

He slid warm hands down my torso, undid my jeans, and yanked them and my panties down to my knees. He spread my cheeks and I could smell myself, strong and sweet with new arousal, faintly reminiscent of the baby wipes I'd used in lieu of showers for the past day.

His teeth sank into the inner curve of my asscheek and I jumped, whimpered, less from the pain and more from the surprise, the desperate feeling that came from the knowledge I'd given my body completely to him.

He asked again if I was a slut.

Forehead pressed to the wall, I moaned and moved my head from side to side. Cold-sweat covered my skin and I could feel the wetness of my slit, the frantic need in my clit. My breasts throbbed with the pain from bruised nipples.

"Yes," I managed.

"Yes? Yes you are a slut?"

I didn't answer, but when he reached up and his nails sank into my nipple, I screamed denial.

"Please…" I begged, struggling to find the right words through tiredness and arousal.

He helped me finally.

"Do you want to be tied and fucked now, cunt? Is that it?"

"Yes," I breathed. God, at last. "Yes."

He didn't insist on a 'Sir.'

I felt him yank my hands down from the wall and pull them behind me. Something dangled against my hands as he brought my wrists together with practiced ease; fabric, but thin like ribbon; shoelaces, obviously. I felt a giddy wave of satisfaction at figuring out that small fact as he wrapped them around my wrists, the rough material biting into my skin with each pass.

I forced myself to take deep breaths then, so I wouldn't pass out as the laces tightened and my heart sped up again with arousal and instinctive panic this time, my brain screaming *Get free! Get free!* But there was no getting free, and that was the great part.

Eyes closed, head still against the wall for balance, I didn't hear him unzip his pants, even though I heard him move. I didn't try to listen. I just waited until he gripped my asscheek with one hand, and I felt him guide his cock between my legs. I shifted, trying to spread my legs wider, rising on my toes and sticking my ass out, anxious to do the right thing and not screw up, frantic to please him with my wet cunt—like I'd always been with him, even before the first time he ever said he wanted to tie me.

I was so wet that it didn't take much trying. I felt his cock press the lips of my slit, felt the fizzle of pain as he pushed deeper; grunted as the breath jolted from me with his first real thrust; struggled to get in another lungful of air before the next. Knowing what was coming and still unable to prepare myself for it. Because there was no way, and never has been any way to make my body do anything but come helplessly when he's fucked me.

That night he used my cunt hard, and with each thrust I felt his belly and the soft hair below his navel brush my fingertips that were tingling and half numb from lack of blood flow. I remember that: an involuntary, forbidden touch despite my bonds. I smiled through the tears of pain from my punished cunt and my aching nipples that he managed to pinch and rub even while he slammed into me. I remember crying when I came: my clit spasming hard under his fingers and forcing real sobs from me.

I think he asked me if I'd come. I don't think I gave a coherent answer.

I do know he slowed down, and told me how good and wet my cunt felt and how he wanted to enjoy it. And I whimpered that I couldn't take any more, but he laughed and said I would take his cock like a good slut as long as he wanted me to. He fucked me slowly, grinding his hips against my ass and kissing my neck and shoulders, and I let my fingers stroke his belly gently, afraid of punishment, but he didn't stop me.

He came like that, pressed against me.

He pulled my panties halfway up and wiped himself off on them and on my thighs before he buttoned his jeans again. The shoelaces, when he untied them, had left red marks across the insides of my wrists. He kissed them. Then he told me to pull my dirty panties and jeans up, and he helped me when my hands shook too much to manage the zipper and the buttons.

I was shivering and he put an arm around my shoulders and held me against him until I stopped. I told him I was sorry, that I hadn't meant all the horrible things I'd said, and he brushed the apology away. He lifted one of my wrists and rubbed it.

"Remember what I told you?" he asked.

I searched my brain for the right thing, second-guessing the answer, second-guessing myself, like usual. But I knew what it was.

"That I'll always be your cunt?"

He nodded and kissed my forehead.

"Get dressed," he said.

A CAMPFIRE STORY

Kristina Wright

I don't camp."

While I looked around nervously at the picturesque setting of endless forest with nary a Starbucks in sight, Nash ignored me and continued to unload camping equipment from the bed of his pickup truck: coolers of food, knapsacks of cooking utensils, rolled-up sleeping bags that had seen better days, and—I shuddered—a tent.

"Seriously, Nash. I know I said I would, but I don't think I can do this."

Nash—a rugged, handsome L.L. Bean poster boy for all things outdoors—had the nerve to ruffle my hair and grin. "It's only three days. You can do anything for three days."

I supposed he was right, but that didn't exactly endear the idea to me. Just because I *could* do it didn't mean I wanted to— or should have to, even if I had volunteered. "You should have gone with your friends. You'd have more fun without me."

"I'm going with *you*. I'm here with *you*." Nash kissed me on my forehead as if I were a child whining for a midnight glass of water. "Now, let's get the tent set up. We're burning daylight."

And that, as they say, was that.

Nash and I had been dating for six months and things were getting serious: serious as in meeting the parents, planning holidays with each other and, now, going on a trip together. While we were frighteningly compatible in a number of ways and the sex was tear-the-sheets and smack-your-mama incredible, we had a decided difference of opinion when it came to how to spend a three-day weekend. I would have been delighted to jet off for a theater weekend in New York City or even rent a cottage by a lake and take leisurely walks along the shore, as long as I could return to a solid building with running water at the end of the day. But Nash liked to rough it: mountain climbing, white-water rafting, off-roading, hiking that required a compass—no GPS for Nash—and a machete. He was McGyver, 007, and an Eagle Scout all rolled into one.

I was pretty sure I was falling in love with him—or I had been before he talked me into an outdoor excursion that was decidedly lacking in the comforts of home. That's how I knew I was falling for him. Every other time he'd suggested joining him in my version of hell, I had deferred and sent him along with his equally outdoorsy, crunchy granola friends while I indulged in a girlie fest of chick flicks and beauty treatments. Not this time. This time, I wanted to go with him—just the two of us—hiking in the woods, camping in the woods, sleeping in the woods. What was I thinking? I was thinking about fucking like bunnies—or bears?—in the woods and had forgotten about all the rest of it.

By the time night fell, fucking was the last thing on my mind. Killing Nash—slowly and painfully—was high on the list, though. After setting up camp (which mostly consisted of Nash doing all the work while I watched since I was utterly hopeless at doing anything except moving stuff from one patch of dirt to another) and a brisk hike through the surrounding woods (which resulted in me tripping over a hidden root and falling in what Nash insisted was harmless undergrowth but which I was convinced was poison oak), we had returned to camp to make dinner. Dinner had been a nourishing combination of meat (hot dogs) and vegetables (beans) washed down by sparkling beverage (lukewarm soda).

Now it was pitch dark and my entire body ached, but I was at least semi-clean. I had just returned from "bathing" at the stream near our campsite, despite Nash's insistence that we could bathe in the morning. I wasn't even thinking about getting clean so we could get it on—like I said, one day in the great outdoors had paralyzed my libido—I just didn't want to go to bed dirty. Wrapped in nothing but one of Nash's flannel shirts and wearing my crazy heavy hiking boots that cost almost as much as my favorite strappy sandals, I focused my flashlight on the ground to avoid another fall. The only place I wanted to fall was into bed, even if it meant crawling into a sleeping bag on the ground of our two-person tent.

As I came out of the stand of trees and into the clearing of the campsite, I could see our tent like a nylon beacon against the unrelenting blackness. I could also hear Nash's unrelenting snores. He had promised to give me a much-needed back rub—and even that hadn't sparked any sexual desire. I just wanted the damned back rub for my sore city-girl muscles. Now it looked like my poor muscles would be sleeping on the hard ground next to the mighty wood-sawing lumberjack. Hot tears pricked my eyes as I struggled into the tent and zipped the flap behind me while my flashlight bounced crazily along the flimsy nylon walls of my weekend home.

It wasn't Nash's fault I was so unhappy, but it sure was easy to blame him at this point—especially since he looked so damned comfortable snuggled deep inside his sleeping bag with only his head peeking out. I stared miserably at my own sleeping bag next to his. He had said something about zipping them together so we could cuddle, but I had refused on the grounds that I would be clean and he'd still be grungy with forest dirt. Of course, he could have just indulged me and gone to the stream. It might have even turned out well. If I was going to suffer like this, I should at least have gotten laid for my efforts, right?

My resentment grew with every contented snore. Here I was, trapped in *Deliverance* territory, and my beloved was peacefully sleeping, no doubt dreaming about an L.L. Bean model who would know how to catch fish with her bare hands. I have to plead temporary insanity combined with heatstroke and malnourishment at this point because all I could think to do was to give him a taste of what I was feeling. Being careful not to wake him, I zipped up his sleeping bag as far as it would go. Then I straddled him, effectively pinning his arms at his sides with my knees. Now he was as trapped as I was. I couldn't help but laugh triumphantly.

Nash's snoring stopped and he opened his eyes to stare at me sleepily. I could imagine what he saw—his otherwise levelheaded girlfriend looking rather crazed in flannel as she pinned him to the ground. Not surprisingly, this seemed to get his attention.

"Hey, babe, what's up?"

I poked him in the chest. "What's up? You want to know what's up?"

He shrugged in his sleeping bag. "Um…yeah?"

I gave his chest another poke. "I like spas. And massages. Like the one you promised to give me."

He shifted in his sleeping bag, suddenly aware that he was zipped in. "Well, let me out and I'll give you a massage, babe."

I wasn't falling for his smoldering blue eyes and tousled, sun-streaked blond hair. Oh, no I wasn't. I punched his shoulder for emphasis, though the thick down protected him from my wrath.

"I don't want a massage!"

"But I thought you said—"

"I want to go home!"

Clearly recognizing I was on the verge of a meltdown and he was in the strike zone, Nash began struggling in the confines of his sleeping bag in earnest. "It's okay," he soothed. "You'll see. You're just tired. Tomorrow will be better. It'll be fun—"

"Will there be sex?"

Nash smiled, falling into my trap. "Of course there will be sex. Lots of hot sex in the woods."

I made a sound like a buzzer. "Wrong answer! There will be no sex! And do you know why?"

He blinked at me, as if afraid to answer. Smart man. "Uh, why?"

"Because you are dirty," I announced. "You are a dirty, grungy mountain boy, and I'm a city girl who believes cleanliness is next to impossible in the fucking woods."

"So I'll clean up in the stream before we have sex," he said.

I could tell he was warming to the idea—he was getting an erection. I wasn't wearing panties and his nylon-and-down-covered bulge pressed pleasantly enough against my delicate bits, but I refused to be distracted. I shook my head, flinging water from the tips of my wet hair. "I won't have sex with some dirty man who thinks dipping his toes in a stream is all it takes to have his way with me."

Nash wasn't smiling anymore. Actually, Nash looked pretty pissed off. "Okay, game's over. I get your point. No more camping trips. Fine. Now can we go to sleep?"

Another poke to the chest and his eyes sparked in a way I'd

never seen before. "I don't think you get it, Mr. Mountain Man. You're not calling the shots here. I am."

"Fine. What do you want?"

I tugged at the heavy hiking boots, struggling to stay astride him. I got them off and tossed them to the far side of the tent, making the nylon ripple. "I *don't* want to wear ugly shoes."

"Oh, is that all?" he said dryly.

Of course, under the ugly shoes were the equally ugly hiking socks with reinforced heels and cushioned arch support. I stripped them off, then stretched one leg out in front of me and wiggled my toes in his face. "And I *don't* want to wear socks. I have pretty feet."

"Well, of course you do."

I didn't like his condescending tone. I wiggled on his erection, reminding him who was in charge. "And I sure as hell *don't* want to wear flannel."

His gaze followed my hands as I unbuttoned his shirt. Suddenly, I realized that maybe taking off his shirt was exactly what he might want me to do. I stopped.

"I thought you didn't want to wear flannel?" He was all but laughing at me.

I gave his cock a little pelvic thrust. "I *don't*, but you might enjoy it too much if I get naked, so I'll keep the damned shirt on."

"That felt good."

I stared at him. I was making absolutely no impact on him whatsoever. "What, this?" I asked, giving him another pelvic thrust. The nylon was slick against my pussy, making it easy to glide along the length of his cock.

"Yeah, that."

"Hmm."

My hips moved against him, almost as if they had a mind of their own. I was getting turned on and while that had not been my original intention, it did seem as if I should make the most of it in this nylon-and-flannel hell. I was on the verge of declaring a truce when he said something painfully guy-like and stupid.

"If you unzip me, you could enjoy this, too."

I stared at him. "I could enjoy this, *too?*" I gave him another pelvic thrust.

His eyes fluttered closed. "Oh, yeah."

"Because," I said, lightly brushing my fingertips along the swell of my breasts under the flannel shirt, "a woman can't enjoy herself alone."

Nash was watching my hands as the shirt fluttered open, oblivious to my words. "Babe," he sighed, as I rolled my nipples between my fingers.

I slid up higher on the sleeping bag, straddling his chest and leaving his dick to drown in down. "Yes, *babe?*"

"You've got me so hot," he said, wiggling inside his sleeping bag like an excited puppy. "I want to be inside you."

"Do you?" I purred, running my hands down between my breasts.

"Oh, yeah. Now."

"Inside here?" I asked, pulling the shirt back and making a heart around my pussy with my thumbs and index fingers.

He stared at my pussy as if it were the Promised Land, nodding intently. "Right there. Deep."

"Like this?"

I rose up on my knees so I could push one middle finger inside me. What had started out as a rant against wilderness to my captive audience of one had turned into something else entirely. It had turned me on. I was soaking wet. I wiggled on my finger, hearing the sexy-squishy sound of my pussy. Nash heard it, too. His eyes went wide as he stared at me.

"Are you going to unzip my bag?"

I shook my head as I pressed another finger into my wetness. "I don't think I need to."

"Don't you want me to make you feel good?" He pressed upward against his sleeping bag and groaned in what I took to be frustration. "C'mon. I'm so hard I'm going to rip a hole in this sleeping bag."

I grinned. "Go ahead."

"*Babe.*"

It was more plea than warning. I ignored him as I slowly gyrated on the two fingers inside me. "Oh, I think you can make me feel good without me unzipping you."

I scooted up another few inches on the sleeping bag until my knees were pressed against his shoulders and my pussy was above his mouth. I stared down at him. The urge to press my pussy to his mouth was almost overwhelming. I felt like if I stayed in this position a few moments longer, I'd be dripping on him.

"Oh, fuck." Nash never swears. Never. I liked it. "*Fuck*, babe."

"You can refuse, of course," I said, enjoying my newfound power. "But I'm pretty sure it won't go well for you."

I slowly eased my fingers from my pussy and showed him the wetness glistening on my fingertips. "Want a taste?"

He stared at me, as intense as he had been when explaining how to shove the tent poles in the ground. "Oh, yeah."

"Good answer."

I rubbed my fingers across his bottom lip. He licked at them, then at his lip. My thighs were starting to quiver, begging to be lowered from this half-kneeling stance. I waited, though, waited while Nash sucked my fingers into his mouth and moaned; waited while he pumped his hips rhythmically, seeking some relief for his neglected cock; waited…until he said what I wanted to hear.

"I want to make you come."

I didn't tease him any longer. Not because I didn't want to or because he didn't deserve it—I did and he did—but because I couldn't stand one more second without feeling his tongue. I carefully lowered myself over his mouth, feeling that first electric zing of pleasure as the tip of his tongue touched my pussy. We both moaned at the same time, as if he was getting as much out of this experience as I was. My knees pinned his shoulders to the ground inside the confines of his sleeping bag in what must have been an uncomfortable position, but Nash didn't complain—and he didn't need anything but his tongue to make me feel good.

I hovered over his mouth, close enough that his tongue could lap at my wetness, far enough that he had to raise his head to get what he wanted. It was a precarious position and I was too turned on to hold it for long, but for the moment I was getting off as much on the expression on his face as his tongue against my sensitive pussy. He groaned, exhaling air across my engorged cunt, and I was lost. I pressed against his mouth then, grinding on his face the way I had been thrusting against his cock, his unshaven jaw scratching at my sensitive thighs. He wiggled his tongue inside me and my pussy tightened, longing for more. I reached down and held his head between my thighs as he dragged his tongue up between my lips and over my clit. He closed his lips around my clit and sucked it gently for a moment before I pulled away and redirected his tongue into my pussy again.

Over and over, I undulated against his mouth, prolonging my spiraling pleasure, as he licked, sucked, and nibbled at my wetness. His entire body surged upward as he buried his tongue between my swollen lips. We moved as one, both of us intent on my pleasure, and I cried out as I clutched at his head. Thoughts of what he could do with his fingers—or his cock—flitted through my fevered brain, but I was too incoherent to release him from his sleeping bag. I needed to come. I needed to come *now*.

"Suck it," I moaned. "Suck my clit."

He moaned against my tender flesh and did as I demanded, sucking my hypersensitive clit between his lips as if he would never let go. The sensation was almost too much for me to take, almost like pain. I whimpered and wiggled, torn between pressing against him and pulling away. But then that fine edge of exquisite torture and unbearable desire blurred into sweet release and I was coming in a gush of wetness. I screamed as I held his head between my trembling thighs, riding out my orgasm against his unrelenting mouth as he made guttural noises and sucked at my pussy.

Finally, slowly, the pleasure ebbed and I curled over him, panting and whimpering like I had run a marathon. I rolled off him onto my own sleeping bag, feeling every bone in my body protest. The flashlight was still on, casting enough light that I could see the wetness on his cheeks and chin and lips. I patted his damp cheek and laughed.

"Wow."

He licked his lips, nodding. "Yeah, wow."

My muscles, sore before our little romp, now felt like mush. "That was delicious."

"Are you going to let me out of this thing now?"

I laughed. "Don't like being at my mercy?"

"It's not that," he said, his voice sounding strained. "I'm naked. And I came."

"In your sleeping bag?"

He nodded, looking as miserable as I had felt earlier. Even in the dim light I could see the dull red flush creeping up his neck. If I hadn't felt so damned good, I might have felt bad.

"Oops. That's not a camping lesson we covered. Whatever will you do?"

He sighed as I worked the zipper of his sleeping bag down. "One, I will never take you camping again," he said. "Two, the next time you want to take a bath in the dark, I will go with you. And three, I will not fall asleep until you do. Ever."

I kissed him, tasting myself. "Always prepared. I like that. Maybe tomorrow night I'll be at your mercy."

"Tomorrow night?"

"Sure," I said, sighing contentedly as I considered the endless possibilities of camping sex. "We still have two more nights, right?"

BEFORE SLEEP DOES

Sommer Marsden

M y Dear Sir,

I couldn't stop thinking about you. Somehow what we did the other night got into my head and wouldn't leave. It seems like forever since we were together, but it's only been two days! And five more days until you come back and we can pick up where we left off. I'm really tired, and it's very hot, and part of me thinks that if I write all of the things in my head down on paper, I will be able to crawl under our white cotton sheets and go to sleep. Once the words are out of me, I can turn the fans on high and drift off to the summer night sounds. Here goes...

You'll notice that I addressed this to Sir. It's one of the things I've never admitted to you—the secret desire that you'll make me call you Sir. Make me submissive to you. I've daydreamed of your telling me how bad I am when I fail to do as I'm told. I imagine it would be really hard to remember to call you Sir when I have never done it before. And every time you address me (in this fantasy), I blunder and forget to address you with respect, forget to call you by the title you have specified. You get so angry with me. I feel my face heat up with a hot shameful blush and I can't seem to stand still. I have to shift and move just the tiniest bit in the small plaid skirt you have dressed me in. My knee-highs seem too hot, and my heels too high, and my stomach bottoms out because I know that I'm in trouble.

"Come over here," you say to me and I can barely move. I've never felt that trepidation with you before. But I do and part of me likes it, likes it so very much that the crotch of my little white ruffled panties grows wetter and wetter with each second that ticks past. "Now. Not when you feel like it. Come over here now."

Somehow I manage to walk over. My knees feel like they're knocking but when I look I see that they aren't. It's just this new and intense anxiety mixed with excitement that has crossed all my wires and made me feel chaotic inside and so very horny on the outside. When you point to your lap, my pussy flickers and I feel the tiny blips of pleasure all through my body. They mix with the fear nicely. I've never been so hesitant and eager all at once.

Your lap, which is a familiar place, seems completely foreign as I drape myself over your knees and wait. It's hard to swallow and it's hard to breathe. I study my long blonde hair brushing the thick blue carpeting. When you lift my skirt, the difference in air temperature is so apparent. My bottom grows cool and when I think that in an instant you will warm it up, I shiver.

You don't give me warning. Not even a grunt or a laugh or a sigh. Your hand lands with a hearty smack and my head snaps back as fire floods my skin and moisture escapes me. "I think you need to count them off so you learn your lesson."

"One, Sir." Before I can finish saying "Sir," the second blow has landed and I'm squirming. Two, three, and four leave me panting like a dog, with my head hanging down and my ass sticking up. I'm not really sure how many you are going to give me and I'm terrified to ask. I don't know if I'm more scared of there being a lot more or the idea that you might almost be done.

"I bet," you say more to yourself than to me, "I just bet I know what I'll find." I start to shake when your fingers explore the outside of my panties. You trace the seam of my pussy with your finger, and I know you can feel the wetness there as surely as I can. You stay silent as you swoop the pad of your finger up and down that cloth-covered slit until I am biting my tongue to keep from begging and clenching my thighs to keep from squirming. My cunt has picked up the tempo of my heartbeat, and it's a greedy, fast rhythm.

Right then and there, I feel like I will die if you don't put some part of yourself in me: your finger, your tongue, your cock, anything. I want to be filled by you in some fashion and I'm terrified to ask and terrified not to. Instead I bow my head and say so softly, "Please."

Your fingers push aside the barrier of my panties and shove into me; two at first and when I hold my breath and then blow it out like I'm drowning, you add a third. I wiggle on them, at your beautiful mercy as you fuck me with your fingers. You know me so well; you keep me right on that edge, walking that tightrope until once again I think I might die.

Your fingers pull free and I don't even have time to protest before your hand lands with a fiery *crack!* and I buck under you as if I've been shocked. "Five, Sir," I cry and six follows so swiftly I add, "And six, Sir, six."

"You're so bad," you say to me and I love it. Secretly I love it. I know I am supposed to act ashamed and I do. And part of me is a bit ashamed for how much this is making me want you. It's crazy even to me how much I want to fuck you, but I love it too. In fact, I love it more than I could ever have imagined.

"I did not give you permission to get wet. I did not say you could get turned on. I think the only thing to do is make sure you really learn your lesson." My breath freezes and my heart skips in my chest. Your voice is full of menace and that makes me break out in goose bumps. You peel my silly little panties down so slowly I can count my heartbeats. Twenty-two heartbeats it takes for you to pull them to the middle of my thighs. They bind me there. I cannot spread my legs, I cannot move much at all. You smooth your big hand over my blazing hot ass and it feels so good. I can't help it. I arch up into your palm. Begging you not to stop but begging you to fuck me, too.

"Take my cock out." I do as I'm told and wait. I know I'm supposed to wait but I don't want to. I am holding your hard cock in my hand and waiting for you to tell me what to do next. "Suck me," you say and I almost say "Thank you," but I catch myself. I take you all the way in, all the hot length of you. I can smell our laundry detergent and your cologne and the distinct smell that is just you.

"Wait," you say. I pause and you deliver the next blow. I must focus not to tighten my mouth and teeth too much or I will bite and if I bite, I'm sure I will pay. "Keep going," you say and I do. But then you laugh. "You didn't say, 'Seven, Sir,' now did you?"

My face grows so hot and I shake my head. A single tear escapes and I clench my thighs and arch my back. Nothing relieves the crazy want and need buzzing under my skin. I just want you to fuck me now. I want to be done with the spanking and get to the fucking. But when you deliver the next harsh blow and the pain sings along my skin and makes my cunt flutter wildly with a pleasure that is nothing but pure potential, I am okay where I am. Okay but still wise enough to say, "Eight, Sir."

"We were to go to ten but I think eleven for the one you missed," you whisper and for just an instant, your fingers are back inside of me, striking that deep place that makes my pussy grow tight and then tighter still.

My body overrides my mind on nine, ten, and eleven. I have your cock in my mouth and your hand on my ass. Pain is skimming along my skin so swiftly I feel dizzy. At the heart of it all is my cunt, wet and ready and just begging for you. So I beg, or my version of begging, finally, laying my head in your lap. "Please," I say. That's it. Please.

You take pity on me, folding me over the seat of the chair before moving behind me. You slip your fingers back inside to test me and I'm so, so wet. "Slut," you laugh and I push back against you wantonly to confirm that it's true. I am a slut for you.

Your cock is impossibly hard and impossibly warm and you slide into me so slowly I think I might scream. I bite my lip instead and focus on patience. It's hard to focus because the friction of your entry had me already on the verge of coming. But that all fades away when you start to move and you are fucking me; blissfully, roughly, fucking me. You yank at my hips and thrust deeper. I can hear my hair whispering over the caned seat of the chair. "Oh, Sir, please," I say again.

You deliver one blow after another to my sore and heated ass. You fuck me harder, spank me harder, and when I come, I'm crying and calling your name. You come with me, which secretly pleases me. I love when we come together.

And that is why I addressed my letter to Sir. I want to call you Sir. For now, though, I will tuck this letter under your pillow until you come home. I hope you find it right away. Until then, I'll think about how it felt the last time you fucked me. And I'll relive this letter in my mind over and over. I know I'll have to touch myself before sleep will come. I will have to come before sleep does. That's fine with me. I'll detail it in full in my next letter. I have a few more days and there's a lot of room under your pillow.

All my love...

BIG HANDS

Teresa Noelle Roberts

One of the first things I noticed about Jim, besides his general masculine gorgeousness, was how big his hands were: hands the size of Texas, hands that could palm a basketball or maybe a planet; hands that looked like they were made expressly for grabbing and gripping and spanking my ass—which was smaller than a planet, but larger than a basketball. I'm not exactly a petite flower.

It didn't hurt that they were attached to someone tall, dark-haired, handsome, and built so solidly he was one loincloth and some archaic weaponry away from being a fantasy barbarian warrior.

Or that said barbarian warrior turned out to be confident and funny and smart.

But the hands were what first caught my eyes.

And I was staring at them now as we lingered over coffee and warm apple crisp (his) and something gooey and chocolaty and caramel laced (mine), reminiscing about the times they'd wandered all over my body—only three, very hot, times so far, but the night was definitely leading to a fourth and I couldn't wait.

Alas, I'd yet to feel those hands doing what I'd been fantasizing about since I first met Jim, namely spanking my ass. We'd survived those three sex dates and a few getting-to-know-you dates before that, though, and I figured I knew him well enough to ask for what I wanted. I wasn't 100 percent sure he'd be into it, but I trusted he wouldn't freak.

But I was sure as hell going to bring it up here, while we still had our clothes on. Just in case the conversation didn't go smoothly.

I took a deep breath, looked around the quiet restaurant, then spoke. "There's something I've wanted to talk to you about. Nothing bad," I added quickly, knowing how men tend to read stuff into *We need to talk*. "It's just that...well, I've got a few little kinks that we might have fun playing with."

It wasn't easy to get out, but when I saw a slow grin blossom across Jim's face, a dam seemed to burst in my panties.

"Funny," he said. "So do I. Just trying to figure out the right time to bring it up. Nothing too hard-core, but I do like a little rough-and-tumble, maybe some bondage."

This was going better than I'd imagined—my big-handed barbarian and I were on the same wavelength.

"How about spanking?" I asked. "Because that's one of my favorite things in the world."

The look on Jim's face was priceless: pure sex combined with a touch of boyish glee. "I just knew... Something about the way you carry yourself." He leaned across the table, whispered, "I'm getting so hard now, thinking about you smacking my ass."

Even through my dismay, I cracked up—it was a laugh-or-cry kind of moment. "I'm not laughing at you, Jim," I managed to say. I didn't want him to think I found his kink funny. "It's just...I was hoping you'd spank me. Ironic, isn't it?"

"Spank you?" He pulled back a little so he could look at me, his expression bemused, but still excited. "That's always sounded hot to me too, but it's not easy to find a woman who'll both give and take…" A little of the confidence left his voice. "And I suggested it to one lover, but she thought my hands were way too big for that. That *I'm* too big. Too overwhelming, she said."

"And that's exactly why I'm attracted to you," I purred. "I like to be overwhelmed."

"Funny, I could say the same. Only in my case, it's being overwhelmed by someone smaller than I am—that excites me a lot. I think you could do a really good job. If you want to, that is. If it turns you on."

We stared at each other, and damn if you couldn't still taste the lust in the air between us, even with this impasse.

But was it really an impasse?

I thought about Jim's big, solid body; about his fine ass in his worn jeans, about how much fun we'd already had, and how much more we could have if we could mutually accommodate each other's kinks.

I pondered what it would feel like to make him writhe and buck underneath me the way I did under a man's hand, to give him that kind of naughty day-pass from the real world. To redden his butt as best I could and then roll him over and ride his hard cock off into the sunset, knowing his tender ass was working against the bed as mine had so often in the past.

To my surprise, my pussy clenched and moistened at the thought.

I can't say the thought of topping a guy had never crossed my mind, as a pure fantasy, but being spanked was just so much fun that I'd never seriously considered switching roles.

At least I hadn't until Jim asked for it.

Maybe it was the way he asked for it so directly—no games, no hesitation. Maybe it was the idea of all that seriously muscled gorgeousness under my power. Or erotic curiosity, wondering what it was like to dish out something I so enjoyed taking. Or that the juxtaposition of strength like his and submission was incredibly hot. Or that I liked him enough to try something new for his sake. Or some combination thereof.

"There's one condition," I said.

Before I could finish, he grinned and said, "Of course. You'll get a turn too."

We made it to my place in record time. His place was a little closer but I favored my place for one reason: once upon a time, my aunt had gifted me with a small wooden cutting board. It wasn't big enough to be useful for much except serving cheese at a party—or maybe paddling someone's ass.

I had plans for that cheese board.

Plans I'd outlined on the way over.

Plans that met with Jim's hearty approval.

I took a minute to appreciate the view. Stripped down, Jim *really* looks like a barbarian hero: dense, hard muscle; broad shoulders and chest; arms that looked like he could pick up a horse; thighs like small trees; and of course those big, hard hands. His cock fits with the rest of the package—he wasn't fully hard yet, but I knew how thick and meaty and downright yummy it would be.

I circled him, running my hand along his heated skin. I considered doing my best bad-action-movie-villainess imitation, just because he so looked like a proud captive warrior who could be tortured but not broken.

I was pretty sure I couldn't do it without cracking up, though.

Probably just as well, because I was willing to bet Jim wasn't all that interested in role-playing, any more than he'd grovel and kiss my feet and call me Mistress. He didn't seem to expect any kind of complicated power games I wasn't comfortable playing.

He was simply a man who knew what he wanted—and what he wanted at the moment was intense sensation on the edge of pain and pleasure.

And that was something I understood: clean, uncomplicated, cathartic, and just plain fun.

Me, I like to be over someone's knee when I'm getting spanked, but no way was six foot six of muscle going to fit comfortably, or even uncomfortably, on my lap.

"Lean over the bed," I suggested. I didn't "order." I don't like being ordered, at least not so early on. Once the play's underway, a switch gets flipped in my brain and suddenly orders can be fun, but I've got to work up to it.

My best guess was that Jim was like me in that.

He bent down, sticking his butt out. His big hands made craters in the foam-core mattress. The position put just the right amount of stretch and stress in all sorts of interesting places—calves, thighs, arm muscles, and of course ass. With his legs slightly spread, I could see his balls dangling. Nice.

"No wonder guys like bending me over," I commented. "It's a great view."

His face looked red. Maybe it was just the lighting, but I don't think so.

I started with my hand, light and stingy. Jim's ass was firm, but his skin was soft and velvety and felt so distractingly good I found myself stopping every few slaps to stroke it more gently. I couldn't imagine that my blows could be doing much, but he was crooning encouragement, pushing his ass out to meet me, and after a while, his skin heated and took on a rosy flush.

"Lovely," I whispered.

He made a noise that was halfway between a growl and a whimper.

I'd known I was enjoying this, but hadn't realized how much until that noise—that familiar combination of bliss and surrender I was more used to hearing torn from my own mouth—hit me straight in the cunt.

I stepped up the pace a little, putting more force behind my smacks, pausing periodically to caress his heated skin, to slip my hand between his legs so I could squeeze and stroke his hard cock (and, I admit, to give my hand a break).

His big hands were gripping at the bedspread, worrying at it. If I'd been able to see nothing but the convulsive motion of his hands, it would have made me hot—I might not have guessed exactly what he was enjoying, but I'd have known he was fiercely turned on.

I kept glancing over to the cutting-board paddle, wondering when to make the switch.

Jim made it easy for me. His voice was as big as the rest of him, normally, but it sounded small as he begged, "The paddle. Please. I need it harder."

One hand resting on his warm butt, I whacked my own ass a couple of times to gauge the effect—which was as stingy and as fun as I'd imagined. (I made a mental note to ask for it myself in the very near future.) Then I turned my attentions back to him.

The first few strokes were awkward, tentative, but it turned out to be easier than I'd imagined to hit my target. Remembering what I liked myself, I made sure to give both cheeks their due, made sure to strike both the meat of the glutes and the deliciously tender sweet spot where ass and thigh meet. That made him jump, like it always made me jump—but, like I did when someone hit me there, he'd immediately stick his ass out for more. Like I did at a similar moment, he made happy noises, shouts, and groans and a keening deep in his throat.

My wrist was starting to get sore, but I could overlook that for a good long time. His pleasure had gotten under my skin and between my legs. I was dripping and aching, but my own desire to be touched, to be fucked, was subsumed by his pleasure, his fierce need.

I'd always thought doing the spanking was all about power.

And I was right, but not in the way I'd imagined. Giving someone the sensations he so craved was headier than I'd ever dreamed. It was yielding to his desires in a whole different way than I was used to, and damn, I liked it.

If he'd wanted me to, I'd have kept paddling him and caressing him until my arm fell off or his ass caught fire from the friction.

Instead, he turned and looked at me with wide, glazed eyes. "Want to fuck you," he said. "Please."

I gave him a few more smacks, said (as if I'd rehearsed it, as if I knew just how to play with his mind at this moment. Which maybe I did, having been at the receiving end of it often enough), "What if I said you had to come from being spanked? Could you do that for me?" I didn't want him to, not really. I wanted that nice, fat cock inside me. But at the same time, I was curious to know if he'd want the other. Sometimes I did…but sometimes, after a good spanking, I just wanted to be fucked senseless.

"Please," he growled, his voice scarcely human. "Please. In you."

And that voice, that edge of desperation and need, finished doing me in. Not that I had far to go at that point.

Just like I'd imagined in the restaurant, he ended up on his back, his hot ass against the bedspread, and even though it's a nice, soft cotton spread, I knew from my own experience that it felt like sandpaper right now.

I knelt over him, rolled a condom onto him, pressed the swollen head of his cock against my dripping pussy—and hovered there teasingly.

At least I did until his huge hands grasped my hips and pulled me down onto him, hard.

He might have been on the bottom, but any illusions I had about being the one in control vanished.

He moved me over him. He pushed up into me, stretching and filling me just about perfectly, hitting all the right places. He was definitely fucking me, not the other way around—and I was not about to complain.

And just about when I was thinking life didn't get much better, Jim began to spank me as I rode his cock.

Okay, so life did get better.

His huge, hard palm felt as great against my ass as I'd imagined, sending jolts of fiery pleasure to meet the ones coming from my clit and my pussy. I'd raise myself to meet his hand, then sink back down onto his cock, grinding myself against his pubic bone.

I wanted to hold back, wanted to prolong the pleasure for both of us, but I couldn't. The orgasm hit me fast and hard.

He continued to spank me as I came, a flurry of light but sharp smacks that pushed me into orbit and made sure I stayed there.

And I spanked him as best I could, slapping at the side of his ass because it was all I could reach. Probably not the most effectual spanking effort, since I wasn't entirely on the planet, but it did what I meant to do: pushed him over the edge so he roared and surged inside me.

When either of us could talk coherently, Jim said, "That

seems like an experiment worth repeating."

Then he took my spanking hand between his two big paws and pressed it to his lips, nibbling at the slightly tender palm until I started whimpering.

What happened next...well, that's another story.

ON THE MEND

Sophia Valenti

Mercy isn't in Marc's vocabulary—and for that I'm thankful. His stern words and strong hand bring me comfort when the world threatens to overwhelm me. It's a blessing that for a few hours each week I can let go of every care and safely surrender to him, knowing I'll get exactly what I need, what I crave. And that's what keeps me coming back for more.

I met Marc at an opening-night party in a SoHo gallery filled with art school grads and Silicon Alley executives. The featured artist was a scruffy photographer whose acquaintance I'd made years ago in a Meatpacking District leather bar. Travis had the same disdain for most of the guests as I did, but he knew that stroking their egos would ultimately pay his rent, so he played the game.

After greeting Travis, I picked up a glass of wine and scanned the room, more interested in observing the crowd than looking at photography I'd already seen. Not only had I seen the photos, I was in a few of them, shadowy shots that were taken the

previous summer in a dimly lit downtown dungeon. The crimson
stripes that had graced my ass that night were artistic strokes of
gray in Travis's black-and-white snapshot of my submission. As
I stood before the image, my bottom tingled underneath my silky
panties, the sight having reawakened the memory of every lash
I'd received. The man who had so skillfully whipped me that
night was gone. We'd broken up hours after that picture had
been taken, which to me made it as bittersweet as it was beautiful. Since that night, I'd stayed away from the bars and clubs.
From time to time, I found myself craving that intensity—the
sensations that would both thrill and soothe me—but I wasn't
eager to encounter another round of disappointment. Travis's
photograph had captured a single, sexy moment, but it seemed
as if the life I'd been living was as frozen and monotone as the
image hanging on the wall.

Shaking myself free from these emotions, I again glanced at
the hipster crowd. They were desperately trying to look bad-
ass in their overpriced designer jeans and brand-new squeaky
leathers, but they looked like children trying to impersonate
older, cooler siblings. I listened to them trying to decipher the
images and impart them with profound, academic wisdom, but
I knew that few of them would ever truly understand the exquisite release that comes from total surrender. While I wanted to
support Travis, this wasn't my scene, but I thought I'd at least
give him the amount of time it took to down a second glass of
wine. However, as I headed toward the bar, I was stopped in my
tracks, mesmerized by the sight of a handsome man who was
chatting with Travis.

I'm not prone to lust at first sight, but this dark-haired stranger
sparked a primal longing in me. His black T-shirt hugged his
sculpted chest, and his lived-in leather pants were equally snug,
highlighting a well-formed ass and muscular thighs. He clapped

a large tanned hand on Travis's shoulder and laughed affably. My eyes lingered on his hand, imagining him wrapping it in my hair and yanking my head back to claim me with a harsh kiss— or better yet, him hoisting me over his lap and spanking me until I came. I squeezed my thighs together, practically feeling his hand connecting with my bottom.

Travis broke me from my reverie, calling out that I should join them. The stranger was staring in my direction, his chocolate-brown eyes seeming to bore right through me. My cheeks flushed as I was overcome by the feeling that I'd been caught doing something naughty, but I regained my composure and wandered over to be introduced to the object of my desire: Marc, the owner of the gallery. I smiled politely and shook his hand, noting how reluctantly he released my fingers from his grip. His appraising glance made my pussy ache. It had been a long time since I'd met a man who exuded that kind of strength and confidence.

Unyielding lust filled my head with white noise that suppressed all logical thought, and I was unable to concentrate on our conversation, although I was vaguely aware of Travis's sly smile as he took his leave, assuring me that Marc and I had complementary interests.

Marc noted my empty glass, gallantly wrapped his arm around my waist, and steered me toward the bar. He didn't ask me what I'd been drinking; he took it upon himself to switch me from chilled chardonnay to the full-bodied red that he'd been enjoying. I didn't mind in the least, savoring its lush flavor.

"Let's get out of the fray," Marc said, placing his hand on the small of my back and directing me toward the back of the gallery. The warmth of his touch permeated the thin silk of my wraparound dress and shot electric sensations straight to my clit. I'd have let him lead me anywhere.

Where he did lead me was through the jovial patrons to a door that opened to an office. When I heard the door snick shut behind us, I felt a quiver of excitement, but I tried to maintain my false appearance of cool as I took in my surroundings. After the chrome and glass décor of the gallery, I was surprised to see modestly upholstered chairs, a leather couch, and an old-fashioned desk, on which sat a brass lamp that suffused the room with a golden light. Music and chatter from the party were still discernable, but it seemed as if we were suddenly a world apart from the crowd. I placed my glass on the wooden desktop, running my hand along the edge of it as I headed toward the picture window that dominated the far wall. I looked through the glass to see pedestrians on the street below and apartment dwellers in the handful of lit windows in the building facing us.

Marc approached me from behind, moving closer and closer until his body was flush against my back. I felt his swollen cock nudging my ass through his pants, and I just barely stopped myself from grinding back against him.

"Travis tells me you like being on display," Marc said, running a hand down my bare arm and leaving a trail of tingling flesh in the wake of his touch.

"Not always," I answered in a whisper, my eyes focusing on his reflection in the window.

With his hands on my shoulders, Marc turned me toward him. He stroked my cheek, then drew his fingers along my jawline until they reached my chin. With a gentle touch, he raised my face so that my eyes met his. "A girl as pretty as you should be on display—for everyone to see."

Marc stroked my neck and continued traveling downward, teasing the side of my breast. I moaned as I felt my nipples grow erect in response to his touch. With a single, fluid movement, he reached down, pulled the tie that fastened my dress and reverently parted the black silk. I remained silent as he slid the garment off my shoulders and let it puddle at my feet.

I glanced nervously out the window, knowing that at any moment one of the neighbors might turn and see me standing there in my high heels and skimpy underwear. I felt my face flush with heat; it was a combination of embarrassment and arousal that I found intoxicating.

"Those are lovely panties, but you won't need them tonight. In fact, no girl of mine wears panties. I require her cunt and ass to be available to me at all times."

"Girl of yours?" I asked, bristling at his presumption. "You don't own me."

"Not yet," he added with a smirk. My jaw dropped as I tried to think of a snappy retort, but before I could form a witty comeback, Marc grabbed my hair at the root and pulled my head back to deliver a searing kiss that surpassed the one I'd conjured in my fantasy. I was still annoyed, but I was also hopelessly turned on.

"A little fire in you. That's good. I'll enjoy breaking you," he hissed in my ear. With his hand still wrapped in my hair, Marc turned me toward the window. "Hands over your head, palms against the glass—now!" I slowly raised my hands and rested them against the windowpane.

I heard Marc tsk in disapproval as his grip on my hair tightened, making me squeak in surprise. "When I give an order, little girl, I expect it to be followed without dallying. We've barely begun, and I already have two reasons to punish you. What do you have to say for yourself?"

I nervously licked my lips. "I'm sorry," I whispered unconvincingly, sounding more petulant than penitent.

Marc delivered a sharp slap to my ass that made me cry out

loud. "I'm sorry, *Sir!* Try it one more time—with feeling."

I took a deep breath as I prepared myself to speak, only to gasp when his hand landed a second time. "I'm sorry, Sir! I'm sorry I've been such a bad girl," I apologized in a mad rush. My silky panties offered no protection from Marc's harsh hand, and the heat of his slaps radiated throughout my bottom and ignited a fierce desire in me.

"That's satisfactory, but it won't save you." Marc roughly pulled down my black undies and slipped them off my high-heeled feet. With my bra and shoes still on, I felt more exposed and vulnerable than I ever had in my life.

I clawed at the glass, listening carefully for a clue as to what might happen next. When I heard the click of a belt buckle and the hiss of leather, my stomach fluttered and I knew. It was everything I feared—and everything I wanted.

I heard the sharp report of leather connecting with flesh, the sound still ringing in my ears as I felt the first fiery stroke of his belt sizzle across my bottom. It was quickly followed by another, and another. With each lash I craved more, even as I debated how much I could actually take. I was thankful that he hadn't asked me to count each stroke because there was no way I could have concentrated enough to follow such an order. My thoughts were jumbled as my mind raced. I thought of party guests hearing the nonstop crack of his belt, of someone wandering into the office and seeing my red-striped ass and thighs, of voyeurs across the street seeing my lips parted in a silent cry as I willingly surrendered to a stranger.

I continued facing forward. Through my tears, I saw a man who was lit by the blue-silver glow of his television. He hadn't realized that there was a more exciting show happening across the street. Part of me hoped he stayed unaware—but another part of me grew excited at the prospect of being seen.

Each time the belt landed, it reawakened the previous strokes, and the heat that permeated my cheeks rapidly spread to my pussy. As my arousal increased, I started to rock my hips provocatively, my body moving in time to the music Marc was creating with the rhythmic snapping of leather. I was lost in his erotic symphony, having been taken past the point of pain.

Whether he thought I'd had enough or he was too tempted by my swaying ass, I don't know. But at some point, he tossed his belt at my feet and knelt between my spread legs. His rough hands massaged my aching cheeks, and his tongue soon followed, leaving cool, wet streaks along my bottom and making my pussy weep. I arched my back to give him better access to my dripping slit, and he answered my silent plea by trailing his tongue along the seam of my lips until he found my clit. He gripped my ass, squeezing my cheeks as he concentrated his attention on my pussy. Unable to control myself, I bucked against his face, the stubble on his chin giving me just the right amount of friction to make me cry out and come in seconds.

I was still panting when Marc got up and stood behind me. "Stay exactly where you are," he growled. I remained facing the glass but seeing nothing as I heard his zipper being lowered and then felt his thick cockhead tease my entrance. He shoved his dick into me in one swift thrust that made me gasp and then lower my head. Marc yanked my hair, pulling it so that I was facing the window again. This time, speared by his dick, I looked across the street and saw that the man had abandoned his bag of popcorn and was staring intensely at us—at me getting pounded by Marc's cock. Having his eyes on me sparked another orgasm, and my spasming sex seemed to trigger Marc's release. His grip on my hair tightened as he groaned and then pulled away from me, leaving my thighs sticky with a mixture of our combined juices as they seeped out of my sex.

Afterward Marc walked me to the couch, where he stroked my hair as I regained my senses, feeling safe and warm in his arms. From the way he cradled me, I knew that he understood who I was and what I needed—that to be broken down was the only way I could feel whole again. And for that bliss, I'll gladly be his girl.

YES, MASTER

Donna George Storey

M y obsession with Major Anthony Nelson was probably
the only thing that kept me going that summer. I'd scored
a supposedly prestigious internship at the State Department—I
dreamed of joining the Foreign Service in college—but my only
apparent diplomatic function was to make copies and file docu-
ments. That and act as a sort of office decoration, because every
time I turned around I caught my fifty-year-old supervisor, Mr.
Lemon, staring at my ass.

A career in the civil service was quickly losing its appeal.

After the long, sweaty commute home, I was ready for some
serious relaxation. So I'd get one of my dad's beers from the
fridge, go up to my room, strip down to my underwear, and
switch on "I Dream of Jeannie" reruns until Mom called me
downstairs for dinner. I'd do a little belly dance to the opening
credits, then settle back on my bed, the cold beer bottle resting on
my chest, to float along with the zany hijinks and comic misun-
derstandings. After a few swallows of beer, I wasn't even really

paying attention to the story. I was just giving old Major Nelson the eye and wondering what the hell was wrong with him. Didn't he have a dick? Here he had this beautiful blonde female ready to do whatever he wished, and all he asked her to do was make dinner when he got home from astronaut training.

By the commercial break, I was still staring at the TV, but I was long lost in my own much hotter show about what those two would really do if Major Nelson had a functioning heterosexual libido. It was all pretty filthy. The Master was always in control, of course, and he'd tell her, "No more blinking and nodding, we're doing this my way." Then he'd take scissors and snip holes in her costume to expose her nipples and blonde thatch so he could caress her naughty parts as she served him dinner.

Next it was off to the bedroom where he'd make her dance and rub her breasts and finger her pussy right in front of him, while he asked her dirty questions—*Is this making you wet, Jeannie? Have you been dreaming of fucking me all day when you were cooped up in your little bottle?* And she'd have to say "Yes, Master," because it was true. Sometimes he'd even make her masturbate with her bottle before he'd give her what she really wanted—his big, heat-seeking missile thrusting inside her. Once they were fucking he'd let her use her powers again to do it in all kinds of kinky genie-only positions. My favorite variation was the "magic carpet" where she'd be impaled on his cock, but levitated with her legs crossed in front of her. With a blink and a nod, she'd twirl round and round on him like a corkscrew until he shot his wad into her with a deep groan.

Of course, all the while I was doing everything the Master commanded, too, palming my tits and strumming my clit, then kneeling on my bed, as if I were straddling him, and wiggling my ass like an exotic dancer. I got so hot imagining his smoldering gaze stroking me like a wet tongue, his soft but stern voice urging me on to greater depravities, that I came with a muffled groan of my own, just in time for Mom's dulcet "Dinner's ready" floating up from the kitchen.

Yes, Major Nelson—or rather *my* Major Nelson, the sexually insatiable dom—sure helped me get through a long, hot summer.

It turned out he was a tough act to follow.

Back at school that fall, I found plenty of guys willing to warm my bed in the usual wham-bam college-boy way, but I still dreamed of the Master. I even splurged on a Jeannie costume and wore it to a big frat party the Saturday before Halloween. Every guy I talked to popped a boner at the sight of my veil and pink harem pants—my first taste of genie power. Only one rubbed my bottle just right, though, a guy named Troy, dressed as Captain Kirk. He looked me up and down and drawled, "Is it true you genies have to grant your Master's command no matter what he asks?"

Unfortunately, once we were up in his room, all he did was shove a beery tongue in my mouth and grope me roughly through the Jeannie bolero. The magic was definitely gone, so I whisked myself back to my dorm and threw the costume in the back of a drawer.

I didn't put it on again until five years later when I met Tony.

Finally, a Master who knew how to do his job right.

It might look like I fucked Tony Rossi from Product Development on our first date, but it was more complicated than that. We'd been having lunch together for months and had flirted pretty heavily through several happy hours when he finally asked me out on an official date to see a play in late October. We had such a good time we ended the evening naked in his bed—no surprise for two people who've been attracted to each other for some time. Except for one thing.

After we were both hot and ready, Tony rolled on top of me, and I thought, *Okay, I'll endure this for a while and then show him how I can actually get off.* But as he started moving this way and that, it actually started to feel...good; very good. It's as if we were having this little conversation with our hips. He'd ask a question, slowly, teasingly. I'd reply with all the right answers, and damn if it wasn't feeling better and better as our lower regions discovered all sorts of things about each other. Until, surprise of all surprises, I was coming, just from old-fashioned missionary-style fucking alone.

I had to see if it was a one-time fluke, so after a reasonable breather, I pulled Tony on top of me again.

Ten condoms and a half-dozen positions later, it was Sunday afternoon and we still hadn't gotten out of bed except to make some coffee and pay the pizza delivery guy. Tony seemed as enchanted as I was.

Unfortunately, reality intervened and he told me he had an early flight on Monday and would be in Pasadena all week on business. However he was anxious to know if I was free the following Saturday.

"Sorry, I'm going to Dana's Halloween party. You know Dana in Marketing, right?" Smitten as I was, I had a strict policy not to stiff my women friends for any guy.

"I was invited, but I was going to blow it off." He smiled. "Do you have your costume yet?"

"I'm going as Jeannie, you know, from that old TV show." I sat up, folded my arms, and did my best imitation of a Jeannie nod. "Yes, Master, you called?" I gave Tony a look that promised everything. "Sure you can't make it?"

His eyes twinkled. "I'll be there."

* * *

I half-expected he might not show. Guys claim they want lost weekends of nonstop screwing, but sometimes that kind of hedonistic excess spells good-bye to any kind of relationship. But he did show up, early, coming up behind me just as I was finishing cutting up pepper strips for the veggie tray.

"Hi, Jeannie," was his greeting.

I turned around. My jaw dropped.

He was wearing an Air Force officer's blue jacket and cap—over jeans, but who could fault him for that?—and he looked rather frighteningly like my longtime fantasy fuck, Major Anthony Nelson.

He smiled at my confusion. "Don't you like me in uniform?"

I was still too breathless, not to mention concerned about a big wet spot on the crotch of my harem pants, to reply, so I simply pointed to his name tag, which read TONY.

"It's a relic from my days at Annie's Pancake House back in high school—sorry it's not regulation Air Force."

"You even have the same name," I managed to stutter.

"Oh, I thought that was intentional...but then I always was a self-centered bastard."

I blushed. I always thought of my old crush as "the Master," not Tony. I did my best to recover with a sultry, "You know I like it when you talk dirty."

His smile widened and he leaned closer. "By the way, that costume of yours is making me hard."

Genie power—at least I still had that card in my pocket.

Just then Jeremy from Finance walked by, his gaze shifting from me to Tony and back. He smirked and gave Tony a thumbs-up. Dana rushed over to take the veggie tray from me, but she stopped short and let out a giggle.

"Hey, you two, cute. *Very* cute."

I suddenly realized that instead of standing there announcing to the whole company that Tony and I were fucking, I'd rather be back at his place actually doing it.

He slipped an arm around my waist. "So how long did you want to hang out here?"

"I'd be happy to get going any time," I murmured back.

We were out of there in the blink of an eye.

When we were finally alone, my real-life and reportedly sexually aroused Major Nelson gave me my first command.

"My dishwasher's broken, so I want you to clean up the dishes in the sink."

Again I was speechless.

"Just do that blinking thing and it won't take long. Let me know when you're done." He walked off toward the bedroom.

I stood in the kitchen, fuming. There were only a few dishes in the sink—a plate with a pair of chopsticks still oily from Chinese takeout, some glasses and mugs—and yet his cocky move made my stomach tight and fluttery with frustration. Was he going to torture me by acting out the real show, where Jeannie and the Master had no more physical contact than a rare kiss?

Still, I dutifully finished my task and crept over to the bedroom door, my heart sinking at the thought I might have a long night of housecleaning ahead.

Tony was lying on the bed, wearing nothing but the officer's cap on his head, bathed in the golden glow of his bedside lamp. The bottom half of him was covered in the sheet, like the drapery on a Roman statue, but it couldn't hide that telltale bulge at hip level.

Major Nelson did have a dick after all.

"All done, Jeannie? I'm ready for my massage." He grinned at me and gestured to the bottle of oil on the nightstand. "While you're at it, why don't you blink and make that top of yours disappear?"

Jeannie as a topless masseuse? My nipples immediately stood at attention. I was still mad at him for the dishes, though, so I decided to take a stand. "You made me promise I wouldn't use my special powers."

Tony laughed. "Why the fuck would I do something dumb like that? You're thinking of that witch show. I want you to use every drop of magic that you've got on me."

I had to smile. But I didn't follow his command.

Tony clucked his tongue. "Take off your top, Jeannie. The few times I watched your stupid program, I spent the whole time hoping your little shirt would get ripped on a nail or something and I'd get to see your tits naked. Now *that* would be worth watching."

My eyebrows shot up. I remembered my own dirty fantasy of the Master carefully snipping away the pointed tips of Jeannie's bra, then chuckling devilishly. My breasts suddenly felt warm and heavy, as if they were yearning for air.

Tony narrowed his eyes ominously. "Take off that top *now*."

My pussy clenched, a sharp contraction hovering between pleasure and pain. My cunt at least was fully in his power.

"Yes, Master." My lips, too, seemed to have a will of their own. I shrugged off the little vest and unsnapped the blouse. I stood before him, head bowed, my pale skin flushing under his gaze.

"Beautiful," he said softly. "Now come over here."

"Yes, Master." I sat on the bed beside him, eyes still lowered deferentially.

"By the way, I like it when you say that. Say it again."

"Yes, Master." My voice was faint and breathy, but there was no doubt I liked saying it, too.

The massage was a more pleasant duty than the dishes. I enjoyed kneading Tony's strong shoulders and biceps, gliding my oiled hands over his flesh. Yet, although he obviously wasn't following his namesake's hands-off primetime policy, my Master had a different method for keeping the sexual tension high.

While I touched him, he was stroking me, too, brushing my breasts lightly with his fingertips, then pulling away for an endless minute before he was back again with another teasing caress. To my disappointment, he carefully avoided the nipples, although he knew mine were exquisitely sensitive. Before long I was trembling with anticipation for the next tiny allotment of stimulation. When he finally gave my nipples a quick flick, I moaned out loud.

"What's this? Do you like the way I'm touching you, Jeannie?" His tone was clipped, military.

"Yes, Master."

"Is it making you wet?"

"Yes, Master." In fact, my crotch was sopping and I was wondering if the cheap costume could stand a washing when we were done.

"I want to see for myself. Put your fingers in your cunt and show me."

My cheeks burned as blood rushed to my face. Guys in my fantasies were always ordering me to touch myself, but I wasn't sure I could really do it. Still, he was my Master and I had to do what he commanded.

I rose up on my knees and snaked my hand into the harem pants. My clit was so slippery and swollen, I almost lingered to give it a few wiggles like in the old days, but that's not what the Master wanted. Obediently I dipped two fingers in my hole then presented my hand to him, palm up.

He gazed at the glistening fingers thoughtfully, then took them in his mouth and sucked them clean.

I closed my eyes, swaying.

"I touch you up here and you get all ready for me down there. That's a great trick, Jeannie."

"Yes, Master."

"It's obvious you're ready to be fucked, which is a fortunate coincidence, because I'm ready, too." Tony pushed down the sheet to reveal his naked cock. As if by magic, it seemed thicker and redder than I'd ever seen it. He reached for a condom in the nightstand.

"I'm feeling lazy tonight, so I'll just lie back and do nothing while you take care of giving us both a good time. Girl astride works better for that, don't you think?"

I hesitated. "I might need a little extra attention to be...satis-fied."

Tony frowned and adjusted his cap to a jauntier angle. "You're supposed to service me, isn't that how it goes? The problem is I really like how you get so soft and squishy inside after you come. So we'll compromise. I'll watch while you get yourself off and then after you're 'satisfied,' you can do me."

I flinched. I pictured myself masturbating in the spotlight of the lamp, Tony's glittering eyes drinking in the obscene show. He was waiting, but my hands were frozen at my sides.

"You look confused, so I'll spell it out for you. First, I want you to lose the harem pants. Then you're going to sit on my cock and play with yourself until you come. Got that, Jeannie?"

"Yes, Master," I replied, my voice catching in my throat. With his wishes laid out step by step, what could I do but get naked and lower myself onto him?

My hands trembling faintly, I cupped my breasts and flicked the nipples with my thumb while my other hand dipped between my legs. My flesh made a soft clicking sound with each stroke of my rock-hard clit.

"Jesus," he whispered. I could swear I felt his cock stiffen and twitch inside me.

Genie power—even without the costume, I still seemed to have it.

I began to move my hips, a slow circling belly dance. Tony was watching me, but I was watching him, too.

I gave him a mischievous smile. "I'm doing everything you commanded, Master, but I'm afraid I'm still being a bad genie."

"Why's that?" His breath was coming so fast, he seemed to be having trouble speaking.

"I'm pretending these are your hands rubbing my nipples and strumming my clit."

His fingers twitched.

I arched back and sighed. "I really wish you could do it for me, but you're the Master and you made the rules."

"Fuck the rules," he growled, rearing up and taking a nipple between his lips. The officer's cap tumbled to the bed. A searing jolt of pleasure shot from my breast to my pussy and I cried out. He grabbed my ass, rubbing it round and round like an Arabian lamp.

There were no rules now and I started to ride him in earnest. Each stroke of his cock drove me higher, up and up. We still had the magic all right because in the next instant I was lifting straight off the bed, spinning, twirling through space. Tony came right along on the flying carpet, groaning and shuddering in release.

When we landed back on the tangled sheets of his bed, we were still floating.

"So what happens now?" he asked. "You granted all my wishes. Do I have to set you free?"

"I don't know. I hope we're on for a few more episodes... Master." I gave him a wink.

Tony laughed and snuggled against me. He was hard again.

Ah, genie power. At first, it didn't work the way I wanted, but eventually I did find a Master who could rub me just the right way. The Master of my dreams.

THE MANIFESTO

Michael Hemmingson

I say, "Tell me about the affair," lying in the dark with her, the cottage warm—the bed warm—*hot*—her cat coming in and out of the house.

"Well," Karin says. "Why?"

"Entertainment value," I say.

"Don't know where to start," she says, and I tell her to start anywhere and she tells me that she thinks it began—at least her affair with this man, who was a photographer, whose name was Conrad Hollis—the day her second play (Karin is a playwright) was to open at the Alfred Jarry. She was walking around downtown, up and down every block, and she happened to run into her husband Kyle who was walking to the Jarry and he asked what she was doing. "Oh, I'm doing my walking thing," she said, and he nodded, because he knew all about her "walking thing" and he said, "Well, I'll see you there," and she said, "Okay," and as he walked away, she looked at him, she looked at his body—he was somewhat overweight and his ass was saggy—and she wondered why the hell she was married to this man, why she'd ever entertained some bizarre notion she loved him, when she never had, and what the fuck was she doing in this city, where he'd dragged her on a whim, and why did she have to suffer because of him? At that moment, that second, she knew she hated Kyle, she knew she never had loved him, and she said to herself, "I *will* have an affair." She said to herself, "I will fuck some man and get back at him for what he did to me." The first person she thought about, standing there on the street, was Conrad Hollis. He was fifteen years older than she, tall and lanky, balding and silver-haired, a thrice-divorced man who dabbled in the arts. She had recently posed for him on a series of breast shots, as had other people around the theater—no faces, no identities, just images of the breast, male and female, the human tit alone or caressed, sucked or espied; in Karin's case, she'd allowed her minuscule bosom to be photographed in solitude, or with a hand cupped below, or a finger grasping the nipple. These sessions before the camera excited her—and it wasn't all the artistic pretensions that Hollis placed on the subject matter, but the mere fact that she wanted to be in bed with the man. Karin had never been particularly attracted to older men—other than some harmless fantasies about a professor or two from college—but she'd entertained some fuck-thoughts regarding Hollis, and walking around downtown that evening, she was determined to have an affair with Hollis.

The opening of Karin's second play went well, most of the seats were filled at the Alfred Jarry, and everyone partied after.

Karin was talking to Hollis.

"You're so pretty," Hollis said.

"Thanks," Karin said. "Do you want to fuck me?"

"Well," Hollis said, "I think so. Yes."

"Then let's get out of here," Karin said.

She knew she couldn't just leave like that, with her husband there. She was drunk enough to make a bold move, so she pulled Kyle away and said, "When we got married, we said—we agreed—we'd have an open marriage."

"Yeah," Kyle said.

"So I'm going home with someone else, okay?"

He wasn't ready for this. He said, "Karin—"

"What?"

"How will I know you're okay?" Kyle said.

"I will be."

"Who? Who is it?" he asked.

"It doesn't matter, does it?" she said. "We agreed, right? This is our marriage, the way we—"

"Right," Kyle said.

She wanted to tell him to fuck off and die, she wanted him to fight for her, to beg her not to go. He didn't. She took Hollis's hand and said, "C'mon," and they left the party and at his car he wanted to kiss her and she let him kiss her; but she didn't like his lips, his tongue, his mouth, his body—

She kissed him anyway and went home with him. He had a two-bedroom house in the suburbs. The sex was okay, nothing to write a ballad about, and when it was over, she thought: *Now I'm an adulteress.*

He had a funny cock, too—it was long and thin and curved like a banana.

She spent the night and woke up before Hollis. She went home. Kyle was eating cereal for breakfast. He didn't say a word to her. She desperately wanted him to say something, to tell her what a bad wife she was, to tell her she was dirty. She didn't feel like a bad wife because she didn't feel like a wife at all; she didn't feel dirty because she didn't feel as if she'd done anything wrong.

Her affair with Hollis lasted six weeks. She saw him two or three times a week.

When she'd leave to see him, and if Kyle was around, she'd say, "Well, I'm going out."

"Okay," Kyle would say.

"I'm probably not coming back until morning," she'd say.

"Oh," he'd go. "Okay."

If he wasn't there, she'd leave a message on the answering machine: "I won't be home tonight." She didn't want him to worry.

And every time she returned, Kyle wouldn't ask her how she was, wouldn't say a thing to her; he acted like she wasn't out having an affair and everything was as it had always been.

The more time she spent with Hollis, she started to understand that he also liked S/M. He was cautious and weary about bringing this up to her—showing her some magazines at first, then a few videos. He wanted to know if she was curious or into S/M. She told him she'd never done anything of the sort, but she was willing to give it a shot. "I'll try anything once," she said. He was very happy and excited about this.

He initiated her into S/M gradually: light spankings on the butt, handcuffing, and blindfolding. One time, he had her squat in an awkward position in a corner of the bedroom for twenty minutes, and all he did was watch her. She complained it was uncomfortable, that her legs started to feel like they were on fire, and he said, "Stay right there like that and *don't* you move." There was something about his giving her an order to be uncomfortable that turned her on. She thought: Is this what S/M is all about, letting go and giving in? She was surprised to discover she also enjoyed that pain in her legs.

Next, he would tie her up and leave her on the bed, not returning for either minutes or hours, she never knew which.

She realized that this was a mental game; the point was that he had complete dominance over her, she was subject to his will and whim. She didn't mind being immobile and captive for a few hours. She could relax and meditate. She would think about plays she wanted to write.

He moved slowly toward her while she was tied, and he had a lit cigarette. She'd never seen him smoke before. She wanted to take up smoking again. She wanted that smoke in her lungs, that filter between her lips. He said he was going to burn off the hairs on her nipples with it.

"Okay," she said. She was excited; she was ready.

There was some pain, but more: there was the anticipation of greater pain, the smell of the sizzling hair, the adrenaline rushing up and down her body, the tingling in her spine and on her scalp.

One night, he was typing maniacally on his Compaq laptop and Karin looked through his stack of S/M magazines, the tied-up men and women, the ball gags, the gimp masks, the piercings, and tattoos. She went to Hollis, to tell him she wanted to try more, like the images in the magazine. She snuck up nehind him and kissed his neck. He jumped at her touch. She asked what he was writing.

"A manifesto," he told her.

She learned that he was creating, in his mind and on his computer, a new religion. She tried reading some of his rantings, but she couldn't follow his train of thought. Something about computers and the new souls inside the Internet, and the year 2014, how micro-blogs were like postcards and the new language of the postmodern was fragmented like news bytes on television. *Whatever*, she thought. Perhaps getting involved with this man was not the best idea—she had a husband at home, after all.

Okay, she told herself, *I have to get out of this affair.*

When she left, she promised herself she wouldn't go back, but four days later, she went to see Hollis again. She also decided she needed a divorce.

It was pretty much the same: Hollis tied her up and whipped her rear end with a cat-o'-nine-tails, and he worked on his manifesto for a new religion late into the night.

She figured: Why not?

BOUND TO ACT

Brooke Stern

B ondage, even when it's happening for real, feels phony. Even with rope burns or bruised knees to prove it, it felt fake to me, like a hackneyed scene read by bad actors. I'm an actress and nothing kills the mood like bad theater.

My boyfriends aren't the types to drop hundreds of bucks on "authentic" (as if) bondage gear or devote square footage in their suburban townhouses to dungeons. Strategically placed eyebolts in the wall above the bed and padded sawhorses made especially for spanking are inventions of perverted webmasters, not anyone I know. Hell, the last time most guys I know struggled with knots, they were sailing or rock climbing, not reenacting *The Story of O*.

My boyfriends were the rock climbing, sailing, downtown loft types. Their vintage shirts say that they can't even wear a dress shirt without irony, let alone hook a leash onto the collar around my neck without cracking an embarrassed smile. They're fine lovers—enthusiastic newbies and still young enough that even when things go too quickly, you don't have to wait long for a second go at it—but some things come with age. These boys are too eager to please to ever treat me the way I fantasize about being treated. They are too thrilled by my tits to ever leave anything more violent than a hickey on them, too busy demonstrating how much pleasure they could give me to think that I might want anything else.

William, though, is old enough to be indifferent to me. It's hard to get him to notice me, even though his acting workshop is four-fifths men and the other women are clearly dykes. Every week, my neckline has plunged toward my ever-rising hemline. I worry that they might meet at my belly button before he notices me. The things he pulls off without the slightest hint of irony—the corner triangle of a kerchief peeking out from his jacket pocket one week, a shirt with mother of pearl snaps and cowboy boots the next—make me wonder if there's anything this man can't do.

When I corner him during break one week, I search desperately for something to say. I remember that he mentioned an impending trip to London. I can think of nothing but Prince William, my generation's newest heartthrob.

"Do you think there are more Williams in England now?" He looks puzzled. "Named after the prince, you know."

"I guess I wouldn't know."

"You weren't named after him, I guess." I'm trying to be funny.

"No. Theater families of my parents' generation named their children after their own heroes."

"Shakespeare?"

"No, darling. Tennessee."

Did he call me darling? I forget to feel stupid.

The rest of the workshop, I marvel at how he can read a script and make it his. It never feels like he is acting. It feels real.

It doesn't matter how bad the student script, he makes it true. I wonder what he would do with my script, the bondage script I have lovingly crafted in my head for as long as I can remember. It was my sexual fantasy before I knew what a sexual fantasy was. It involves restraint and degradation, leashes and whips, and the relief of unspeakable urges.

The last workshop comes and almost goes, and I still can't write the script for his seduction of me. Can't he just do it himself? What am I missing? I stay after, waiting while all the ironic-shirt-wearing boys clamor for an introduction to his agent or an internship with his company. I invite him to coffee. He agrees but seems caught off guard, as if the thought hasn't even occurred to him.

I know the neighborhood around the theater and make sure we go to a place with a liquor license. I order wine, but he is unwilling to follow, sticking to coffee, as if it's written into the script. He isn't cold, but he seems elsewhere. He hasn't even loosened his tie. The longer it goes on, the crazier I get. He listens patiently as my talk goes from professional aspirations to personal hopes to childhood reminiscences and recent heart-breaks. My god, can I sink any lower? He has broken me open with nothing but his indifference.

I should hate him. I should leave and preserve whatever dignity I have left. But instead I order my fourth glass of wine and hope he didn't notice the tears that I can't keep from gath-ering in the corners of my eyes.

"I have to pee," I say, the wine and my urge for a moment's respite finally getting the best of me.

When I put my hand on the table to support myself as I stand, his hand clasps it firmly and holds it in place.

"No," he says. I am halfway up but sit back down. "You've earned it. Why don't you enjoy your reward?"

What? He has dropped a fifty from his pocket on the table and is leading me out to the street, and I am still wondering if I've heard right. He pulls me by the hand. We are headed back in the direction of the theater.

"How badly do you have to go?" he asks.

"I don't have to go." Does he think I have a curfew or something? How young does he think I am?

"How badly do you have to pee?"

Oh. We are passing the theater. It was locked up hours ago, but maybe he has a key.

"Badly."

It isn't really that bad. I could wait. But I don't want him to take me home. An abandoned theater suddenly seems perfect, but we walk past and turn into the dark alley by the stage door.

"Do it."

"What?"

"You could be good, you know?"

I was more confused.

"You could be really good. A star. But you need to let go. You hold it too tight. You work too hard."

I've heard this before, but no one has ever been able to fix it.

"Let it go."

"I've tried. I can't."

"A minute ago it was badly, now you can't?"

"You can't mean…"

"Do you want to learn a lesson?"

"Yes. I mean no." Is it a threat or a promise?

"This could be yours."

He gestures to the stage door, the private egress opposite the green room for those too recognizable to use the rear entrance. I am confused, disoriented by thoughts of stardom and degradation all at once, by his warm praise and his sharp orders.

"Mark your territory."

That is what sends me over the edge. We are in the script. I am feeling it. I will do it. I will do whatever he says. But then I can't do it. I squat down halfheartedly. I reach up my skirt to pull down my panties, but I hesitate and stop. He won't take his eyes off me. Suddenly I don't have to go at all.

"I can't."

He takes off his tie and walks over to me. He ties one end of it around my neck, tight enough that I feel pressure all around, and ties the other end to the railing at the stage door. The railing is low and the tie isn't long enough for me to stand straight up. A gentle push and I am down on my knees on the hard cobblestones. He takes off his belt and wraps it tightly around my wrists and then around the bars on the railing. The belt holds me awkwardly and the leather bites into my wrists.

"I can wait," he says when he's tied me in place.

I try to raise myself off my knees and squat, to at least look like I am trying, but I can't get my balance. Then I try to raise myself up so that I can pull down my panties with my bound hands. It is hopeless, but I hope he might see what I need to do and help me. He doesn't take the hint.

"My panties..." I say.

"What about them?"

"I can't..."

"So?"

I looked down. He has me. It is just like I want it. I shift a little on my aching knees and feel the tension of silk around my neck and the strain in my shoulders as my arms are awkwardly torqued. I won't be able to stand this much longer. I think about the four glasses of wine and close my eyes but being in public, being watched, kneeling, and wearing panties all conspire to make it impossible.

"I really can't…"

"Can't what?"

"I can't let go."

"Let me show you."

Without his belt, it takes him no time to unbutton his jeans. I strain at the tie around my neck to suck him as best I can. He is rough, pushing my head and pulling my hair as he pleases. I am growing increasingly uncomfortable and try everything I know to get him off as quickly as possible, but he stops me periodically and holds my head still even as I try to keep sucking him.

I become desperate, stiff and sore in my bent joints, bruised and tender where all my weight rests on my knees, and occasionally stifling a gag when the tie pulls hard at my neck. I work harder and harder but to no avail.

"You first," he finally says. I know what he means. I close my eyes and it takes a minute but I finally let myself go, feeling my panties soak through and then the puddles forming at my knees before I feel his throbbing in my mouth. I am wet everywhere: my legs and feet, lips and chin.

He uses the toe of his leather shoe to lift my skirt and peer underneath at my panties, the fabric darkened and still dripping. I look up at him, unable to wipe my face but proud of my state and of what it symbolizes: my letting myself go and playing the role that I had always fantasized about. He unbinds me and I rise stiffly. I reach up under my skirt to pull off my panties. They are soaked and I am going to leave them there, but he stops me.

"Leave them on," he says. I blush at the thought of walking down the street with wet panties. "You can wash them at my place."

I look back at the puddle where I had been. In the morning, it will smell like every other alley in the city. Passersby will curse the homeless and the theater personnel will write it off to some psycho fan, but it is mine, now—every bit as much mine as if I had exited that door and stepped into the waiting limo on opening night. That will happen, I think, but in its time. Now, it's time to go back to William's place and wash my panties.

DEAL

Shanna Germain

*H*earts

Slap, slap, slap go the cards across the big wooden tables. The wood's so old and used you can't see the grain anymore, just the layers of acrylic in primary colors, the dark stains, the etched promises of eternal love and hate. Below the hand I'm being dealt, *Sherri True Love Forever's Bobby* in black sharpie, her *TLA* interwoven as though that alone would make it true. *Andy* carved his name in *'98*, or maybe it was earlier and he was merely scratching his hope that by '98 he would be allowed to leave this place.

This place was once an art room. For the underclassmen, it still is, I'd guess. Earlier in the year, it was for us too. We'd walk around with our cameras hung from our necks, snapping shots for the darkroom, our fingers smelling always of chemicals, our pupils dilated from the constant change of light. But now it's April and our cameras sit forgotten beside our elbows. Graduation is upon us like wild dogs, and we can't think, much less be creative. Our teacher merely watches us from his desk, reading art magazines with half-naked women on the covers. He's been through this before. He knows that for us seniors, eighteen, some nineteen although they don't want to say it, it's no longer about brushing gesso over canvas to prepare a proper medium or pounding clay into the table until the gray chunks become part of the grain.

Now, it's about this: euchre. I don't know where we learned it. Someone moved here and brought it and now we all know the rules: fast cards, jack's high, bower, follow suit, trump, shoot the moon, win tricks. It's the language of the space in between.

We play euchre in school, and we fuck out of school. Our obsessive brains ignoring classes, college fears, hopes for the future in exchange for something quick and unthinking. I dream of cards and cocks, of plays and ploys. I hear the shuffle in my sleep and wake with a start, fingers itching to curl a hand around them, the sworded queen inching across my sheets. The one-eyed jack come to fuck me and make me his.

The slap-slap of cards stops, and I bring my five-card hand facedown toward me across the bumpy table, peer at it without raising my eyes to my partner on the other side. My partner is also my boyfriend. Daniel. Redheaded, with soft green eyes that puppy-dog me if I'm gone for too long. Nice boy. My dad likes him, talks Zeppelin and Syracuse basketball when we go to my house.

When we go to his mom's house, Daniel fucks me with his fingers in his bedroom while she's at yoga. He fucks me with his cock on the nights that she's got her book club, those nights when she comes back late, a little drunk, a little talkative, and sniffs the air before she takes me home. I've never tasted his cock, although I want to. He pulls me away every time, begging off, saying it makes him feel bad to see me like that.

Daniel always uses a condom, rolling it on with shaking fingers before he slips his thin cock, like a finger itself, like a finger crooked in a "come here" gesture. And then he climbs on top of me, pushing carefully between my thighs, holding himself above and off of me like I'm one of the big-bowled, breakable wine glasses his mom drinks from. Asking if this is okay, if this hurts, if he can go a little harder.

Gentle and slow, is what I write in the journal that I keep locked and stuffed into my desk drawer, hidden beneath stacks of old paintings, from when I still used to actually do art in art class. *Sweet,* I write. "Sweet," I say, when he asks, swallowing the word as though it's anything but.

Clubs

I slip my cards up, fan them between my fingers. My hand is stacked with clubs: jack, king, queen, nine. Clubs: that dark black shape like a deformed hand or a heart being squeezed to death, like a cluster of mushrooms; not a single red. I try not to think of the cards like this, as some kind of sign. They're just cards, just one hand out of many. I'll get another one as soon as this is over.

Dropping my cards back to the table, I wait to see what happens. Euchre is played with two teams and the team we're playing against is Kim and her boyfriend. Her boyfriend, improbably named Biff, a name that even more improbably actually fits his wide shoulders and near-blond buzz cut, taps the edge of his cards against the table on my left, a signal I've come to know as meaning he thinks he's got a good hand. He's asking Kim not to trump him, to let him lead. Kim doesn't seem to pick up on this cue, ever. She looks like a cheerleader, all blonde and blue-eyed, but she plays wild and slap-shot, as though she's always shooting solo. She calls trump, ignores the low look in his eyes when she takes the card into her hand.

Euchre is a fast game: don't think; react. Or, ideally, think and react at the same time. It's like learning to drive. At first, you have to take the time to do both. Think *turn right* and then you do. Think *stop* and then you do. But after a while, it happens at the same time. That's euchre too.

Kim called, so she starts off. She flips her card to the center of the table, over a scarred *Angelina <3s Dougie:* queen of hearts. I throw one of my black cards, the ten. Biff tosses his too, an ace, as though he hadn't just been overtrumped by her decision.

Slap. Slap. Slap.

Pause.

Daniel plays slow, waits for me on every move; doesn't lead unless he's got an incredible hand, which happens once in never. He scans his cards, the pile at the center, the score, my face. I wonder what he reads there. Can he tell I don't have a single red card for him, neither diamond nor heart?

While we wait, I dig my nails into the hollowed letters of *Andy '98*—all those circles, round and round, soft edged, eternal, sweet and slow.

Kim watches my finger. She doesn't like me, doesn't trust me. She thinks I'm making a sign to Daniel, these incessant circles. When she thinks I'm looking at my cards, she watches me with her pale eyes behind her petite glasses, pushes a bleached curl of hair off her forehead with an exasperated blow of air.

She shouldn't like me, shouldn't trust me. I'm fucking her boyfriend. Or he's fucking me. Not that she's caught us. Or that she can see his knee edging to push my thigh open beneath the table. She can't see the signals Biff flashes as they play the game—or else she just openly ignores them—but she can see something in the way I touch my earlobe each time his hand slips beneath the wood to draw a few nails roughly over my thigh. Or in the way I close my cards into a single pile when he touches the camera strap, long and lean and black, that snakes over the scarred wood, slithering as he pulls it between his fingers. It's the camera strap he used in the darkroom the first time he kissed me, dropping it over my neck to pull me toward him, his mouth clean and stringent as the developer that dripped from my thick black gloves.

We kissed for a minute, maybe two. It's hard to say in the dark if time speeds or slows. At the end, he said, "Suck me." Probably the only thing he'd ever said directly to me. Suck me. And oddly, I did. Going down on my knees on the darkroom floor, letting him open his jeans with one hand and hold himself for me. I ran my tongue over the smooth head, surprised it tasted of the clean dirt of mushrooms, same texture, only smoother. He leaned down with one hand pulling my gloved hands over my head, curling his fingers around my wrist to hold me there. With the other hand, he pulled the camera strap tighter around my neck, forcing me over him, until I was gagging either from the width of him in my throat or the black strip of fabric wound against my windpipe.

He bucked into my mouth, pulling the strap tight until every thrust was a flashbulb popping in my brain, until I was exposed, exposed, all my edges, all my hidden suits brought to light. When he came, I swallowed, the liquid draining down my closed-up throat. Behind my eyelids, my veins captured the dance of safe-lights, rough-edged reds. After, in the bathroom, I saw the pale strip of darkened skin across my neck, like a line of diamonds, a winning hand, pointed edges cutting my skin.

Diamonds

Finally, Daniel slips his card slowly over the ridged table: diamond, king of. Bad card, bad choice. If that's the best he's got up his sleeve, we might as well end it now

Kim pushes the stack toward Biff—his win—and he throws down his opening card. We wait. Again. For Daniel.

I watch his bare fingers tap the card backs, the freckle on his pointer knuckle. I drum my own bare fingers, ringless, one, two, three, over my cards.

Daniel has asked me to marry him. We had sex on his bed first, the way we always do, his cigarette mouth on mine—that inhale of ash his only vice—as his freckled knuckles disappeared inside me. Then his so-pale-that-I-thought-it-should-be-freckled-too cock sliding, entering slow, curving upward like a finger. I closed my eyes and thought of the taste of mushrooms, lifted my chin toward him, asking his hands to do something I didn't know how to say. He kissed my neck, lips so soft they barely registered, and then he pulled out as he came, holding the base of the condom with one shaking hand.

After, he got down on one knee at the side of the bed, his eyes the same color as the blue comforter he'd wet with his come. I wanted a cigarette, still needed something in my mouth: unsatisfied lips, hungry tongue.

Instead, I got his hand catching mine, a shiny circle in his palm.

"Marry me?" he said. The same way he said *Is this okay? Can I enter more?*

"No," I said.

"It's a real diamond," he said, as though that mattered, as though that might make me say yes.

The diamond he's laid down on the table is a real diamond too; the wrong diamond, the wrong suit entirely. The other diamond, the one in neither of our hands: I wonder where it is now.

Spades

Kim lays down trump with a sound that's nearly a squeal. As she gathers the cards—her win—Biff's knee touches the inside of mine, his hand dropping to grip hard enough that later I will have three small black bruises on my thigh.

The first time we fucked, really fucked, Biff bent me over the developing table loaded with deep trays filled with chemicals, my hair nearly falling into the developer. My own unfinished photo was in there, waiting for me, forgotten as Biff pulled my jeans barely down far enough that he could kick my legs apart, yanking a dry coil of uncut negatives from the wall. "Arms back," he said. Is it awful that I knew what he meant, like that, my hands clasping behind me? Is it worse that I wanted it, the way he wound the negatives around my arms, cutting my skin with their paper-sharp edges—how he curled a second one around my throat, over and over, holding to the end of it like a leash?

"Bend more," he said, and I bent while he gripped my bound wrists with one hand, the leash around my neck with the other, his cock slipping into me so fast I hadn't realized I was wet. I bent so far I could see the details of the photo: me and Daniel sitting on his couch. His mom took it, after. I watched it darken a little more with each thrust, each rasped breath slipping beneath Biff's tightening hands, until I closed my eyes and saw only the red of my veins and the safelight—coming with a shattered suck of breath, my first time. Pop. Pop. Pop. The flashbulb, the slap of cards, a winning hand.

Only later would I notice the ends of my hair, split and shattered by the chemicals. Only later would I notice someone else had pulled the photo from the tray and hung it up to dry. In the black and red of the darkroom, you couldn't even see the tiny diamond resting on my hand.

Deal

"Trump," says Kim, and she pulls the cards from the center like a greedy child. It's their win. She gives me a look, then leans across the table to kiss Biff. It's a soft touch, a graze of lips that makes a sound like dry paintbrushes. I have to dig my fingernail into someone's forgotten *loves Cary forever!* and dip my head not to smile.

Daniel collects the cards and shuffles, the slow chirrup of faces falling on each other. Biff cuts the piles with one hand and drops the other below the table to pinch the inside of my thigh. I know I'll have marks like diamonds, scattered along my skin. Kim gets the first card, facedown. I get the second. The card lands on *Jesse+Connor*.

It's anybody's game.

WON'T YOU BE MY NEIGHBOR?

Rita Winchester

M r. Rogers was the first neighbor to greet us when we moved into the neighborhood. "Frank Rogers. Your neighbor. Hold the jokes," he had said in that very soft but commanding voice of his, and smiled. He had ash blond hair shot with gray, cut short but not military short; pale blue eyes that brought to mind faded denims worn and loved. Mr. Rogers was pretty damn buff, too, something I never failed to point out to Jessie.

"He rides that bike Monday, Wednesday, and Friday like clockwork," Jessie had laughed. He turned our steak on the grill and then glanced over the fence to make sure Mr. Rogers hadn't heard.

"Grocery story on Friday nights," I laughed. I sank into the lawn chair and sipped my now-tepid beer. "Dry cleaning comes home with him on Mondays."

"He puts the trash out at four fifteen precisely every Thursday," Jessie said. "Spread your legs," he said softly, so only I could hear.

I did. I let my legs fall open in the lawn chair. My body pointed toward my husband and his smoking grill—but also pointed toward Frank Rogers's house. No panties under my knee-length paisley sundress. I was bare and shaved and suddenly wet. Warm summer air blew up my dress and over my bare pussy, licking at my clit with a phantom tongue. "Like that?"

"I wonder if he can see you?" Jessie said, snapping his barbeque tongs my way. He started to hum the song to *Mr. Rogers' Neighborhood* and then came to stand before me, his hard cock, buried under his old faded shorts right at my face level. "Won't you be my neighbor?" he singsonged softly.

I laughed and he promptly removed the steak, hauled me inside, and fucked me senseless, humming that ridiculous song as he made me come and then come again. And when he came he barked, "Neighbor!" before chuckling softly and kissing me hard.

Then we ate dinner.

Three weeks later, Jessie announced his business trip. We sat on the porch as dry lighting lit the sky and the heavens rumbled threateningly. But not a drop of rain fell. I sipped my beer and watched Frank Rogers drag his cans out to the curb. He stopped, gave an enigmatic smile and a single wave. We both waved back and Jessie leaned in. "We must not deviate!" he said with a nod to the trash cans.

I laughed too but then felt bad. "Hey, he's precise. He's... demanding of himself...in control. He's organized."

"He's fucking OCD is what he is," Jessie said and finished off his Corona. "Maybe that's why he's not married?" He frowned and cocked his head. We heard Frank's back door bang and my husband grinned. "And that would be him out to water the garden. Water every day except days with rain."

"But take Sunday off," I snickered. Because it was true. Mr.

Rogers watered every day unless it rained. Sundays were off, though, to prevent root rot. He'd told me so one day, his handsome, tan face serious; his eyes only straying once or twice to my tits in my thin white eyelet dress. It had turned me on, him looking at me that way. But I hadn't told Jessie and I didn't plan to. He'd just make fun. To him, Frank Rogers was a joke. To me, he was intriguing.

"Must not deviate!" he said again and went inside.

When I turned, I found Mr. Rogers staring at me as he watered his roses by the side fence. I sucked in a breath, mortified and embarrassed. He shocked me by winking at me. It wasn't an older man next door wink either. It was more of a *I'm going to fuck you senseless if I get ahold of you* wink.

Or I had lost my mind.

When Jessie left two days later, I felt an odd excitement buzzing in my belly and lower. I had become obsessed with that wink. I practically shoved Jessie out the door after about a dozen kisses and an almost fucking in the kitchen.

"God, baby, I'm going to miss you," he said and swooped in for one more kiss.

"Me too," I said, and it was true. I would miss him. I loved my husband very much. But in my mind, as his tongue danced over mine, I was being gripped by the upper arms by a very authoritative and rigid Frank Rogers who would then push me to my knees and order me to suck his cock.

And dear god, I would. I would do anything he told me to because that was how he was, a commanding man who made you hold your breath just a bit to see if you passed muster. I pushed Jessie out the door after one more kiss and when his car was gone, I threw on one of my many summer frocks and a pair of black flip-flops and off to the garden I went.

It was four thirty. Mr. Rogers worked in his garden from four forty-five to five thirty on sunny days. I sank down near the fence and started to pull weeds, my ass in the air, my back bowed. I could hardly breathe. The fifteen minutes I had to wait ticked by like years. I was ready to scream, throw my spade, go crazy when I finally heard Frank's back door bang the way it banged almost every summer day.

"Nice day," he said, inclining his head as he walked past.

I nodded back. "Mr. Rogers," I gasped like a schoolgirl and put my face down. I was blushing so hotly I thought my face might slide right off between my emotions and the hot sun.

"You look hot. Are you hot?" He did not address me directly; he said this to his tomato bushes. For every one straggly tomato bush Jessie and I had, he had five huge, vibrant bushes. His garden was lush and green where ours was sad and defeated.

"I am hot." Each word weighed on my tongue, so heavy I felt like I was pushing coins off past my lips one at a time as I spoke.

"Lift your dress a bit. There's a lovely breeze."

It was not a question, a request, or a suggestion. He was telling me to do it. I did it. I hiked my pale lime-colored cotton dress up so that the hem was only half-covering my ass.

"You wore panties," he said to his squash vine. His pale blue eyes did not find mine. Not yet. "That's odd for you. When you're out here, it's usually bare naked cunt under a soft flowing dress. You were feeling shy today," he said.

Then his eyes did find mine and my heart did a drunken little jump in my breast. I nodded. I had. I had felt shy and white cotton panties has been my defense.

"Take them off," he said, bending to grab the hose at his feet. "Put them on the fence post." He gave the garden a soft spray.

I shimmied out of them and scurried through the soft green

grass to hang my panties on the post like a surrender flag. I was about to turn around when his hand shot out and he grabbed my upper arm, squeezing. Electricity soared through me and my pussy went wet. I was so scared and excited my pulse beat painfully hard in my temple. "Sir?"

"Come over here. You can help me tonight. I have some things for you to do."

I glanced around me as I hurried to the adjoining gate, a very simple red wood gate between Mr. Rogers's yard and ours. The perimeters of both yards were contained with six-foot privacy fences. We should be shielded. No one would see us, but the prospect that they might gave me a secret, sickening thrill. The gate squeaked just a bit and then I was in his yard. It looked so different from his side than from mine.

I walked to him, stood behind him, waited. He did not turn but said, "Come stand in front of me."

I did. I stood there, facing him but not looking at him. My heart beat quickly and I realized I was holding my breath. "Get on your knees and pick those few weeds. No matter how careful I am, a few always get past me."

I sank to my knees, pulling the three dandelions and a tiny bit of clover. His crotch was level with my face and I could smell his soap, something clean but peppery. "Look at me."

I looked up. His face was kind and handsome but serious as hell. "Unzip me."

My hands were all over the place as I complied. I had to shut my eyes to steady my heart. He pulled his own hard cock out as I knelt there in the thick green forest of his successful summer garden. "Open that pretty mouth of yours," he commanded.

I opened wide, letting his shaft slide past my cherry lip-glossed lips and over my tongue. He tasted rich and dark like a summer night. I started to hold his hips, so I could get him deeper, but his voice cut through the excitement. "I want your hands crossed behind your back. We don't have anything to bind you but the image is the same. Mental and otherwise."

I did as I was told, kneeling on my haunches, hands crossed at the wrist behind my back as Mr. Rogers started to fuck my mouth. His hands burrowed in my short blonde hair, and he tugged here and there to sharpen the pain. Everything seemed loud and big and bright kneeling there. I could feel a root under my knee and a leaf tickling along the back of my calf. A bee buzzed by my ear and it sounded like a helicopter it was so loud. I sucked him hard and I tried to relax my throat to take him deeper. His lean hips pushed at me, banging his cock to the back of my throat.

Then he said, "Stop."

But I didn't want to stop. I was just finding my rhythm and my cunt was so wet. I was right there, in that place where I am as turned on by the act of the blow job as the man getting it. "Now!" His voice dropped but his hands yanked and tears flooded my eyes as I froze. Great waves of pain sizzled over my scalp. I clenched my thighs and moaned, hidden there in the green leaves like a garden fairy.

Tears streaked down my face but I realized my mistake. I had not listened and that was unacceptable. Frank knelt in the grass, gathering a shoot from a squash plant that was thick and gnarled, its yellow bloom fragile despite the hairy texture of the vine, wrapping my wrists and bending me over. "Panties and disobeying. You have so much to learn. I'm not surprised, though. Your husband is so undisciplined. And you too."

I heard him cut something and realized what it was: a thick dried vine, long dead. They streaked the fence, his side and ours, and no one had bothered to cut them. Thinner than a pencil but stronger than rope, they were ugly but invisible in the foliage of the backyards. When it bit into my left asscheek, I bowed in reverse prayer. Head tossed back, face to the blue, blue sky as if in plea. "Oh, god!" I sobbed.

"Talking will only make it worse," he said. I quietly cried through nine more strokes with the dried vine. Because he said I had to. So I would.

I hung my head in the dirt. My tears made wet divots in the sandy earth as Frank smoothed his big calloused hands over my hot, welted skin. My vine-bound hands in front of me, I moaned again, pleasure covering over the pain like a balm as I felt his fingers push at me, into me. He was parting me and filling me and finally fucking me as I kept my ass up and my head down. Now when I cried it was due to the immense sense of goodness flooding through me.

I pushed back against his hand and bit my tongue to keep from talking. Talking would make it end. It was all about obedience. If I anticipated it too much, if I wanted it too much, he might take it from me. I steadied my breath and waited. The hot, smooth head of his cock pressed at me and I had to focus not to strain back against him—to force him in, to force my will. Forcing my will would mean I would get nothing.

I could see that now.

"Such a good learner," he said softly. "I see you trying so hard. So, so hard. Good girl. You are a fast learner. I can tell you and I will get along just fine."

The head of his cock pushed and bumped the sensitive places in my cunt that screamed for attention. I tightened around him, orgasm speeding toward me like a violent storm. I whimpered, watching my hair trail in the dirt. His fingers played and plucked over my fragile skin. He circled my clit until I shook with the sobs and then he fucked me hard, holding my hips and bucking against me until I crashed down around him, sobbing hard into the dust as he mastered me.

He pushed a finger deep inside of my ass and said softly, "So pretty," as his hips bumped faster and faster. Finally, the Master surrendered to his own pleasure, all the while humming, *Won't you be my neighbor...*

A LESSON ABOUT GENDER

Xan West

For F., who inspired the initial incarnation

From the first time I saw those boots—big, black, obviously steel toed—I was mesmerized. But what got me were the ragged metal fangs around the ankle, not quite teething the leather. Unabashedly a bootlicker, I was captivated by the challenge that his boots posed my tongue. From the moment that I saw him spank her harder than hell with that strap, making sure it hit close to home with role-play based on her stint in the army, I knew. From the moment I saw the boy? dyke? serving him as he topped her, it was definite: I wanted to know him; not just him, I wanted to know all three of them.

So when I was there in the dungeon still floating after my scene, and I saw them playing, I had to watch. I was rooted to the spot. And I realized watching him...with his girl...with his boy...how utterly gendered D/s can be, not just for me, but for others as well.

With his girl it's intimate, reaching into all those places instinctively guarded, so dangerously deliciously intimate, his blade menacing her eyes, piercing the inside of her lower lip. She's bound, revealed, facing the voyeurs; intensity building; then silky sliding penetration, fear twisting into pain. She's tough. It's not about breaking her. It's about ripping her open slowly, savoring each tear, each exposure, each soft sound. She's trembling, uttering very few words, simply soft gasps and pleading eyes. He's up close, very close. She's slowly split open like fruit, tears dripping.

With his boy: the boy's not bound, not still. He takes positions braced against hardness: hard wall, hard floor; back to the crowd for the entirety, physical distance between them. Sir is huge, towering over his boy. He's using percussive, slow rhythm; simple tools: fists, boots, belt; punching, kicking, beating, jarring. The boy is required to hold positions, made to do push-ups, pushed to physical limits. There's constant verbal interaction, the boy's voice keeping rhythm, counting off. Tears are present, but they're not the point. Fear is not the point. He's tough. It's not about breaking him. It's about building him up, revealing his strength to him, building something important, the boy taking pride in himself, Sir taking pride in his boy.

It was gorgeous to watch, both scenes, all the way through the aftercare to the end when they kissed those amazing boots. There was something that seemed so gendered about their play, it captivated me completely, created possibility. And when he let his girl out of the cage where she had been watching him top his boy, and she said, "I will never get the pronouns confused again, it is so completely different," I was floored. Because that's exactly where my mind went. Topping a boy is utterly different from topping a girl. And I realized how amazing they were, those few Dominants that had seen and celebrated me in my multiple genders.

More than anything, it made me miss you. You were the best at it. You could spot a gender switch before it was even conscious. You never got my pronouns wrong, even when I switched back and forth several times in an evening. You just knew.

I miss being your girl. I want to give it up to you again. I want to be spread wide and plundered. I want you inside me, devouring me, ripping into me. There is nothing like giving it up to you. Nothing that pushes me farther, nothing that feels more intimate, nothing as intensely holy.

When I gave it up to you, I found a place of deep focus, to the exclusion of all else. In some forms of meditation, they say you should find your center. When I was your girl, giving it all up to you, you became my center. That's what made me want to be your girl in the first place.

At my core, what I really want is to float away, to find that dreamy place where my will is aligned with yours; where I am helpless, hemmed in by my own choices; where every moment that I face my own desire to stop this right now is another moment to choose to give it up to you. And you kept presenting me with that choice, over and over and over again, until those moments layered onto each other and surrounded me with chains of my own making, chains that set me free of distraction, free of my busy brain; free of today's stressors and tomorrow's fears, free of everything but that moment of choice and the wave of bliss it builds. I knew that then you would take what you needed from me. Then you would delight in devouring me. Then I was yours.

Sometimes you chose to take me with pain, to unleash your sadism onto me. If I close my eyes, I can still feel your quirt on my skin. You would lay me across the table and tower above me, slamming those thin strips of leather into me until I stopped writhing and began to float. At some point I would just find stillness.

That's when you would bring out the canes and lay lines of piercing sting onto my skin. The strokes would build in waves of pain and I could ride them forever. By the end, you would be a snarling ravenous leopard, your claws raking me, your teeth driving into my shoulder, your cock reaching so far into me it felt like I would burst.

Sometimes you would choose to take me with control. You would demand ownership of my body, your voice writhing inside me, fisted around my will. You loved to force me beyond my threshold, to push me until I was sobbing as I came.

You would lie down and make me ride your cock, your hands dispensing pain as you ordered me to come for you, again and again. Every time you drove your teeth into me you would make me come. You would cover my mouth and nose and grab my eyes with yours as you forced me to come for you without breath to sustain me, repeatedly, until it felt like my head would explode, until I was dizzy with pleasure.

You would ram my cunt down onto your cock, an evil smile on your face, telling me that I could not stop, that I was yours to fuck, yours to control; that my holes were yours, my pleasure yours, my orgasms yours to dispense or withhold.

You would force me until I was sobbing, begging you to stop, until I was sure I couldn't take any more orgasms. You would force me until it hurt, my cunt battered and throat sore from screaming, face and chest soaked with my own tears. Then you would grab my nipples in your fingers and pinch so hard it was like your hands were made of steel, and order me to come one last time for you, come as you rammed into me, riding out your own pleasure.

I loved being your girl. I miss that surrender. The thing that was so amazing about you was the way that you could turn on a dime, the second you saw me shift. And sometimes, you could even coax me into the gender you wanted to play with. When I was your boy, I felt so strong, so grounded. When things were hard, sometimes you'd coax boy into me so I could tap that strength.

I always seemed to breathe deeper when I was your boy, to take up more space. I felt more whole. If girlness was you being my center, boyness was being my own center. As your girl, my core was open and vulnerable, but as your boy, my core was stubborn and strong. When I was your boy, my pride was in my toughness, my utility. I was so proud to be your boy, because in being your boy, I proved how useful I was, how much I could endure. I proved it to myself and to you. Each bruise was a badge of strength, each completed task a sign of my determination.

As your boy, I was able to tap a deep faggotry that had been denied realization by a trick of biology. There was no disruption in it for you. You fully celebrated my raunchy queer sexuality. I could sink into it with you, hold none of it back, know you would meet my faggotry with your own.

Sometimes it was about proving I was tough. You would beat me with fists and boots, floggers and batons, repeatedly, relentlessly. You would pound into me as I stood tall, chin out, proving I could take it, that I was strong enough. I would clench down on my jaw, push my boots into the ground, and endure. Deep bruises would grow on my skin, my muscles would tighten against it. And still it would go on.

When I was your boy, I felt like I could endure anything. You pushed me farther than anyone, and I loved you for that. Each blow brought me deeper into my body, built me up taller. You were pounding pride in with your punches. By the end, when you eased your hand into me, magnifying your efforts until you began to punch-fuck me, I felt so full, so sure. It was joyous when you pounded your fist inside me, intense, almost indescribable. I was amazed that I could take it, that it was so fucking good. I felt so loved, so strong, so whole.

Sometimes it was about being useful, hard physical labor that left me sweaty and determined. I would gut my way through my body's protests and finish the damn job. There was so much pride in that, in knowing I had endured it, pushed myself through it. Being offered as a bootblack for a community event, blacking the boots of everyone, no matter whether they deserved my skill, even the presumptuous assholes, even the ones who brought me boots so destroyed it made me want to cry. Blacking boots until my hands ached, my arms felt like spaghetti, polish smeared on my skin, grim purpose on my face as I serviced pair after pair of boots.

You were always my last customer, a test of my determination. I would push my body to take the care your boots deserved, savoring the sensation of the leather under my hands, the scent of the polish, the sound of your groans as I rubbed your sore feet through the leather. When I lay on my belly to lick them, time stopped. If I close my eyes, I can taste them now, feel your boot heel pressing the back of my neck, holding my mouth onto your boot. Licking your boots was like sucking off your dominance, servicing your power in a visceral queer way.

Afterward, you would drag me to the bathroom, push me to my knees, and force your cock down my throat, your hands holding my head still as you rammed into me, praising me for being such a good cocksucking boy. You would shove your cock into me, groaning as I choked. The entire time you fucked my face, you wore a wicked grin and filth spilled out your mouth.

Just when I thought I was going to pass out if I wasn't able to take a full breath, you would pull out, bend me over the toilet, bare my hole, and drive your cock into my ass. Nothing made me feel more like a faggot than being fucked in the ass in a public bathroom. I reveled in it, smut streaming from my mouth as I begged you to use my ass, fuck me raw, ram yourself so deep inside me I could taste it. It felt so free to get fucked that way.

You would order me to clamp down on your cock with my ass, praising my strength, and I felt so randy, so queer, so boy. When you came, and I felt you spurting into me, I knew my worth, and was sure I had pleased you. That was what would make me come, secure in the knowledge that I was yours.

You were the best at reading me. You could see right into me, knew exactly how to wring one more ounce out of me, push me just a bit further, possess me thoroughly. Sometimes at night, the back of my neck aches for your touch. I miss being yours.

DO I LOOK LIKE I'M JOKING?

Annette Miller

One of the hottest times I've ever had with my husband was when he tied me up in a movie theater. I am not making this up, but I still kind of can't believe I did it. You know those cherished sexual memories you keep in the back of your mind and bring them out when you want to get really turned on really fast? This is one of mine, probably my very favorite.

This encounter was actually our second time getting dirty in this very movie theater. The place was a rep house showing foreign and independent films, and in enough financial trouble that even though the movies ran morning till midnight there were a lot of empty seats and a lot of darkness.

It was in a college town an hour from our house—far enough away that we probably wouldn't run into anyone we knew, which was prudent of us.

The first time, Jim and I made out, and I had given him head at an 11:00 P.M. showing. Then, the whole back half of the theater was empty. It was so fucking exciting to both of us that even though I'd given him head to completion (is that a polite way of saying it? He came in my mouth…) we went home and immediately fucked.

But for Jim, even pushing the edge of safety like that didn't satisfy him unless there was bondage involved. Jim's a serious devotee of the rope and leather arts, and after a bit of a nervous start I've learned to seriously appreciate them as well. When it started, I quickly learned that Jim tying me to the bed meant that I would get made love to like a princess and come and come and come. It happened a dozen times and from that point on when Jim said, "I'd like to tie you up tonight," my answer was almost always, "Yes, please!"

When he wanted to change things around and tie me up but make me service him, instead of my just being bound and pleasured—I immediately went wet to the knees. I know it sounds insane, but that sort of thing had never really occurred to me. When Jim cuffed my wrists and put a collar around my neck and grabbed my hair and pushed me to my knees—all right, I was a convert. The bastard made me as big a pervert as he was.

And I'd already done a dangerous, illegal, and probably immoral thing by giving Jim head in the theater. Was I really surprised when my husband wanted a repeat performance, but with his very favorite hobby incorporated?

"Now it's your turn," he told me. "You're going to come in the theater, tied to the chair."

"You're joking," I told him.

"Do I look like I'm joking?"

Oh, I had a million objections: Jim overrode them all. "We're doing it," he said, playfully, and I was secretly glad that he wanted it so badly—it meant that the fear fluttering in my stomach seemed a little less daunting. I'd do it to make him happy. How fucking wet it made me wasn't the point.

* * *

This was maybe six weeks after our first encounter in the theater. We went there for a late-night showing, but when we showed up this time it was not nearly as empty. We had chosen a French movie that was legendary for having lots of sex in it; in fact, word had it that it was mostly an excuse for sex. I won't tell you which movie, but it was a truly filthy one, just this side of being XXX-rated.

There were people all around who were just barely old enough to be going to an X-rated movie; like I said, this was a college town, so I figured these were mostly students. But Jim wasn't turning back. "We already went this far, let's give it a shot. If we get in trouble we'll leave."

I wore an overcoat to the theater because underneath I had on a little dress that didn't leave much to the imagination, and I was wearing both anklets and wrist cuffs that are obviously restraints but can double for fashion statements. They were not fashion statements in this case, though; Jim intended to use them.

I did not wear much underneath the dress so it would be nice and easy for Jim to get to whatever he wanted to touch. Just knowing what we were about to do made us both feel so dirty, and we had barely waited for the movie to start before Jim got his ropes out and tied me to the theater seat. The leather cuffs were padlocked, and so once Jim had me secured there wasn't anything I could do.

"I think I'll go get a drink," he said with a devilish smile.

"Don't you dare!" I hissed, but he chuckled. It was within the boundaries of what we had discussed; I was welcome to safe-word if I wanted, but of course I wasn't about to; just being tied up like this in public was making me incredibly wet. I could feel my clit throbbing under my tight dress, and every time I rocked back and forth I could feel my smooth clit rubbing against the lace of my thong.

Jim carefully draped my coat over my lap, careful to cover my wrists so nobody could see they were bound to the theater chair. My ankles were exposed; had an usher shined a flashlight, he would have seen the ropes and cuffs. Just knowing that made me wetter.

Jim got up and went into the lobby; he took his sweet damn time getting a drink. The opening scene played—sex, of course, though I was in no condition to read subtitles. A number of groups of latecomers came by and looked like they were going to ask if the seats next to me were taken. None of them seemed to notice that I was tied to my seat, but nonetheless none of them decided to sit next to me. Who knows what they noticed? The possibility excited me and made me feel guilty for being excited. This was getting dangerous.

When Jim came back he had an extralarge drink. He offered me some by nuzzling the straw into my mouth; I tasted whiskey, and lots of it.

"You're so bad," I mumbled around the straw.

"You don't say," he answered.

I was nervously thirsty. Jim held the cup with one hand, sipping and offering me some periodically. His other hand drifted under the overcoat, up my dress, and down my thong.

He started to finger me, absently, me trying hard not to moan as he worked me into a frenzy. Being so nervous made me even more thirsty, so I sucked whiskey and Coke and pretty soon I was pretty buzzed. Jim's hand worked as the action unfolded slowly on the screen; there was an arty, '60s-style sex scene every ten minutes or so, fairly explicit. I was squirming nervously. I fought against the cuffs and ropes holding me to the theater seat. I started to get pretty sure I was going to come. That's when Jim popped the top off the soda and fished out a few pieces of ice.

"Don't you dare!" I hissed.

He just put his mouth up against my ear and whispered, "Don't want anyone to hear you...."

He reached over with his cold hands and popped both of my breasts out of my tight, low-cut dress. I was not wearing a bra. This was not under the overcoat, mind you, but in full view of anyone who troubled to look in the back row. My head swam and I swear I could have climaxed right then, just from the blush that ran through me for fear of being discovered. Fear, and excitement—part of me wanted everyone in the theater to turn around and see what we were doing.

But the theater was just barely dark enough that nobody around us seemed to notice. I felt so exposed—horribly, terrifyingly exposed, which excited me more than I'd ever been excited in the past. But I was bound to my seat and Jim was in control; I let him be, the arousal washing over me as he teased and tormented me.

He began to work the ice against my nipples and I could not stifle the gasp that came to my lips.

"Shh, be quiet," he said. "You don't want everyone in this theater wanting a piece of you, do you, you little whore?"

It always gets me started when Jim calls me dirty names like that, and I was already well past started. My nipples were alive from the touch of the ice, painfully hard and throbbing and aching. I kept looking to see if people around us were noticing; either they were clueless, trying to be discreet or, as was the case with many of them, they were too involved in their own make-out sessions, many of which seemed to involve wandering hands. My nipples are exquisitely sensitive, especially to ice, and Jim got me good and worked up before he kissed me deeply and gave me a deep slurp of whiskey-cola, and then got enough fresh ice out of the cup that I knew exactly what he was about to get up to.

"Oh, god," I whispered. "Oh, fuck oh, my god—don't, don't, don't…"

His ice-filled hand went sliding up my inner thighs, and when I tried to close my legs he growled, "Open them or I'll tie your knees open too."

I fucking went wet inside; the idea of being bound with my knees spread open there in that theater was more than I could stand. It turned me on so much that he didn't have to tie me, though; I imagined it vividly and felt my thighs spreading wide as if he'd magically bound me there.

Then his hand filled with ice went up to my crotch and I felt him plucking the crotch of my lacy thong out of the way.

A powerful gasp erupted from me as he touched the hard ice to my clit. I whimpered into his neck and felt him bending down to warm my nipples with his mouth as he froze my clit. The sensation was intense. He teased my clit as I struggled not to make noise; then the ice went into my pussy. It felt like I melted it in an instant, but my pussy tightened around the ice. I looked around desperately to find out if people were watching us. Some were: two men down a few rows in front of us. I was scared by their gaze but both of them were smiling.

Jim saw them, too, and smiled back. He kept stroking my clit, leaning in close to me so I could smell him, feel him against me, taste the whiskey-cola when he kissed me deeply.

"You ready to come yet?" Jim whispered.

"I don't think I can," I murmured.

"You can," he said firmly. His hand came out of his pocket holding a little vibrator, the size of a quarter or smaller.

"Oh, Jesus," I purred. "Oh, fuck…"

I knew this vibe well; he had used it to make me come once

at my parents' house, while we shared a bedroom we weren't supposed to be sharing. I knew well that the hum of the vibrator was quiet enough to make me feel safe at home; it would not make me safe in public. No vibrator was quiet enough to prevent me from feeling exposed, frightened—and incredibly turned on, knowing others could see and hear.

"Think about all these people," he whispered. "Watching you. Hearing you come."

The two men a few rows in front of us were both still watching, smiling, one bearded, older; one smooth-faced and young, both sitting alone.

"They're watching," said Jim. "Listening to you come. Come for me. Come for *them*."

Did I mention I'm an exhibitionist?

I'm far from shameless but utterly predictable, and Jim knew that's exactly what it would take to get me off despite my embarrassment.

He switched on the vibrator and slid it up my skirt, down my thong, and pressed it to my clit.

I caught my breath and tried not to moan. I bit my lip. It didn't work. I moaned. He pressed harder. His fingers sank into me. I was so incredibly tight from having taken the ice that it sent a shudder through me. I moaned louder; I couldn't stop myself.

"I'm going to come," I whispered.

"Really," he said. "With all these people watching?"

I came, surging and bucking against the theater seats. I was bound to them and I felt like I'd never been bound more tightly. In front of us, the two men knew exactly what had happened. They watched and smiled silently.

Jim finished me off, kissed me, and tucked my breasts back into the dress. A guy with a red flashlight entered. He started going up and down the rows. He looked at us suspiciously, but passed us by.

"Did you come hard?" he asked.

I nodded, unable to speak.

"Are you ready to pay me back for all the nice things I did for you?"

I found my voice: "Oh, my god," I whispered. "Here?"

"No, not here," he said.

I breathed a sigh of relief.

"There's a great park not far from here. You can pay me back there. People watch there, too. It's all the rage in England, I understand, but it's a new thing here."

"You're joking."

"Do I look like I'm joking?"

He leaned down and used a pocketknife to cut the ropes that bound me.

I made it to the car on wobbly legs, and I more than paid my husband back.

IF YOU WANTED TO

Diana St. John

Middle finger upright, as if with a mind of its own, flipping you the bird; that's how this started. You couldn't possibly have known the other day at work when our verbal barbs escalated to their normal crescendo that something inside me had changed.

You couldn't have known the inner tension, the stress, the interior attitude pushing you, teasing you, bratting you as best I could in the midst of an ordinary day, wishing you knew the code I was trying to share; that I longed for you to crack, willing you to know what was at stake, wanting you to turn the tide of control. You couldn't have known I was begging you to put me in my place, wanting you to be my master.

But you could if you wanted to.

And when you laughed that rich, deep, wonderful laugh you have and looked at me intently for that instant, eyes searching, testing, commanding, you wouldn't have known that I sometimes wonder if there is indeed another tone underneath the laughter, a tone that might hold a promise of threat; a veiled, "You'll pay for that...."

But you could if you wanted to.

You certainly wouldn't have texted me later with a message short and sweet telling me what to wear, where to meet you, and a time.

> *white sundress w/poppies. red patent pumps. red*
> *thong. no bra. hotel on s. main, rm 412 @1900.*

You wouldn't have issued these commands stated as facts with the sure knowledge that I'd be instantly wet, achingly needing to obey.

But you could if you wanted to.

When I arrived to let myself into the empty room and paused for a moment in the bathroom to freshen up, you wouldn't have left a note propped up by a bottle of bubble bath on the tiled counter next to a gleaming metal-handled razor with instructions to take a few moments to relax before paying particular attention to shaving myself for your pleasure, making sure to remove every stray hair from the soft skin of my mons all the way down to my tight pink sphincter.

But you could if you wanted to.

You wouldn't enter the room quietly as I soaked after having diligently followed your instructions. You wouldn't silently step into the bathroom to catch me off guard. Certainly you wouldn't just gaze at me, watching my nipples poke up through the fragrant bubbles, hard from the chill in the air. Hard because I was just that fucking turned on, lost in the role of being your toy, lost in the pleasure of submitting to you, wondering just what you might be planning to do with me, to me. You wouldn't see me taking my hand from the water and tracing my fingers

down the soft lines of my face, my neck, down the curve of
my breast and the obscenely engorged nipple, tweaking it once;
sliding my hand down the pale peach skin of my belly and the
velvety soft skin of my freshly shaved cunt; circling my clit with
my middle finger and teasing those soft lips open, the slippery
wet fluid of my arousal so evident, so much wetter, hotter, than
the warm water of my bath. You wouldn't notice the pads of
my fingertips stroking my lust-swollen pearl, faster and faster
as any consequence of climaxing without your prior permission
was overtaken–I'd be so turned on I simply had to come right
then. And you wouldn't stand there in the doorway and chuckle
appreciatively as my moans of enjoyment gave way to my impossibly loud yells of climax, enjoying my flush of erotic embarrassment when I realized you'd been watching me get off.

Of course, you wouldn't just flat-out ask me if I had been
masturbating, if I just couldn't control myself any longer; if it
was the actual shaving of my pussy that had made me wet or just
that I had done it because you told me to. You wouldn't tell me
that you'd long known before we had ever talked that under the
disguise of "woman in control" I wear at work there's a naughty
girl who longs to give up control and who sometimes wants it
fiercely ripped away.

But you could if you wanted to.

You wouldn't have helped me out of the tub, not allowing me
to dry myself but toweling me yourself, using the towel not too
gently on my nipples, the insides of my thighs, my newly sensitive and bare labia, my clit, awakening them with the roughness
of the towel, leaving me hungry for more.

But you could if you wanted to.

You wouldn't have known how to suddenly snap your
fingers and point to the floor in a form of practiced communica-
tion between us, knowing I would instantly be kneeling down

on the cold tiled floor, sitting back on my heels with my knees spread, eyes down, submissive—*your* submissive.

But you could if you wanted to.

And you certainly wouldn't have known to bring out a narrow chocolate-brown collar with a ring in the center to fasten around my neck, taking my breath away with the sudden gesture of ownership, communicating to me that in this time, in this space, I was yours to do with as you pleased. It's unlikely that you would have run your fingers through my hair and pulled my head back, forcing me to look in your eyes and see the power, lust, and tenderness mixed so powerfully in your own eyes. You wouldn't grab the ring and tug, forcing me up to my feet, pulling me into the next room, directing me to lie face-down, spread-eagled on the bed, waiting, while you stood casually and observed me trying to quiet myself, still the pounding in my heart and in my sex.

But you could if you wanted to.

You wouldn't have given the command, "Present," expecting an immediate response on my part, knowing the way I hate the fact that I love that particular position, on my hands and knees, my back to you, legs spread, upper body supported by the bed, holding my asscheeks apart; exposing every bit of myself for you, that you might observe, inspect, or use me for your pleasure. Or any combination thereof.

But you could if you wanted to.

I'm sure you wouldn't have examined my attention to detail, the thoroughness with which I had followed your instruction to shave myself well, particularly around my sensitive pink anus. You wouldn't tease the tight, never-penetrated opening with the tip of your finger, or quickly remove your hand only to bring it down sharply, delivering an unexpected spank to that most sensitive sphincter.

But you could if you wanted to.

You wouldn't inform me that I had missed a hair or two—maybe truthfully, maybe more as a mindfuck to obliterate the sense of control my perfectionism gives me. The sense I have that by following directions perfectly, I still have the upper hand. I wouldn't argue, knowing as I would that quibbling in such a position would merely bring your disapproval, along with strokes of the cane, the former being harder to bear than the latter.

But you could if you wanted to.

You wouldn't have reached for the shaving cream and razor, enjoying my shiver as you worked the cream around my asshole, teasing me once again, pressing your finger into my ass ever so slightly before taking the razor and, commanding me to stay still, used short, firm strokes to shave that most private of areas.

But you could if you wanted to.

After you finished and used that same rough towel to remove the last traces of shaving cream, you wouldn't announce that that the time had come to deal with my rude comment and gesture earlier in the day, and you certainly wouldn't produce a most unexpected sound, the unmistakable click of a pocketknife being opened and used to whittle something, out of my eyesight.

While I might not have been able to see it, the scent of the ginger root would have given your intentions away, and in my mind I'd be protesting—you couldn't possibly have been planning to do that which I would realize without a doubt you were preparing for. You couldn't possibly, I'd think, just before the freshly peeled piece of ginger penetrated my anus, warming and tingling from the inside, its spicy heat radiating contagiously to my pussy.

But you could if you wanted to.

You wouldn't then calmly state that you were going to

spank me until you were sure I was sorry for my earlier impulsive gesture, sitting on the edge of the bed and gesturing for me to assume that familiar, embarrassing, damnably erotic position over your lap, ass ready to be tenderized by your strong, powerful, yet comforting hand.

But you could if you wanted to.

When the first spanks landed, hard and unrelenting and stinging much more than first spanks ought to, so early on, I'd think that you couldn't possibly—or maybe you could have and did know how much more exquisitely sensitive a spanking is on skin still pink from a nice warm bath.

And when I started to squirm and writhe, trying to move my burning ass out of the way of the onslaught, grind my throbbing pussy into your lap, and raise my bottom up to meet your hand all at the same time, you couldn't possibly have known how your growled threat to stay in position, coupled with the volley of spanks to the sweet spot where my asscheeks meet the top of my thighs caused a new flood to gush between my legs and the throbbing in my clit to match the rhythm of the spanking, again and again.

But you could if you wanted to.

And when the heat building in my ass became too much and I started grinding into you again for relief, you wouldn't stop, use my hair to pull me to my feet as you stood up and arranged a stack of pillows at the edge of the bed before pushing me back down over them, ass high in the air.

But you could if you wanted to.

And no, of course you wouldn't, you couldn't reach for the implement that causes the greatest interior turmoil, the most un-PC implement, the one I shouldn't want at all but am instead most embarrassed to admit makes me nearly climax at the sound and the scent, let alone the feel.

Of course you wouldn't, I'd think, until the sweet sound of the leather coming through your belt loops made me near crazed with desire; you couldn't possibly know how I want, no I need to hear it, to smell the leather, to feel it licking like a tongue of fire across my ass, my thighs, and even up between my legs, lapping at my pussy.

But you could if you wanted to.

And you couldn't know that the fiery heat building inside my ass from that sliver of ginger, combined with the repeated and inescapable molten-hot burning delivered by that sweet strap of leather across my bottom, thighs, and cunt would work their magic, would rip away any and every sense of being in control in a most visceral way. You wouldn't have known that this would make my breathing change, become more ragged, as the sweet release, catharsis, and climax that only this sweet pain can give danced infuriatingly close and I could almost reach it.

But you could if you wanted to.

You couldn't possibly know the effect that it would have if you decided to drop the belt and take a moment to unzip your jeans, pulling out your cock. I might think and hope you were preparing to fuck me, not that you'd stroke your deeply engorged cock with one hand while using the other to slap my cunt, spanking it again and again and again as you jacked yourself off. You wouldn't possibly think of fucking with my mind like that, of adding the humiliation of making me merely the canvas to hold the artistry of your seed as it released and sprayed across my skin, in the ripping away of ego I so desperately need.

But you could if you wanted to.

You wouldn't possibly know how I would climax, over and over, or perhaps just one long orgasm, as your own release erupted from you, hot semen against my hotter flesh, a growl deep in your throat and your whole body as you ejaculated against my back, my ass, my thighs. You couldn't have expected the sound of the energy deep in my throat, an animalistic sound: pleasure, pain, release, and relief even intertwined with tears as the energy ripped through me, blasting any last illusions of control into a hazy glow as we collapsed onto the bed, bodies still pulsing from the intensity of it all.

No, you wouldn't have known any of that as your eyes held mine intensely for a moment and you laughed that wonderful, deep, rich laugh that seems to hold such promise, such desire to take control.

But if by chance you ever decided you wanted to, you could.

MY FAVORITE GAME

Dakota Rebel

My brain felt completely fried by the time I drove home from work. It had been a wicked week, ending with an even worse day. I just wanted to get to the house, pour a shot of something hard and cold, and put my feet up until my husband got home from work.

When I pulled onto our street, I was surprised to see his car already in the driveway. I was glad he was there, but I couldn't help wondering what he was doing home already as I unlocked the front door. When I saw him sitting silently in the living room, elbows on his knees, staring at me standing in the doorway, I knew.

The terrible day was washed away completely in a full-body shudder at the sight of him, in that pose, with that look on his face. He saw my reaction, smiling wickedly at me in response.

He stood, walked over to me, and kissed the tip of my nose. I smiled, then cast my gaze to the floor. He chuckled, the sound low and deep in his chest. I struggled not to look up at him, not to meet his eyes before permission was granted for it.

His hands found my hips, turning me violently to bend me over the coffee table. The front door was still wide open, but I dared not say anything. I just took a deep breath and planted my palms flat on the table. I waited for him to shut the door, but he didn't. He moved behind me, pressing against me hard enough that I could feel his erection rub against the crack of my ass. I shifted slightly against it, which earned me a sharp smack with his hand on my bottom.

I didn't sigh, but I wanted to. Instead I dropped my head lower, hoping my hair would hide the smile that had broken out across my face, hoping he wouldn't stop if he knew how much I wanted this today, how much I wanted him right now. Sometimes if I showed him my happiness at the situation he would remove himself from it. That was always the worst.

Today, however, I seemed safe from that. His hands slid down my thighs, wound themselves under my skirt, and then rose up again, lifting the fabric and baring my ass to him, and to anyone who happened to walk by the house. Though after one good swat to my naked bottom I didn't care who saw me, who saw *us* and what we were doing. It didn't matter so long as he didn't stop.

Of course, he did stop. A whine escaped my lips when my skirt fell down my legs again. I clamped a hand over my mouth, but it was too late. He had heard me. He placed a finger under my chin, tipping my face up to look at him. He shook his head slightly, a disappointed look in his eyes. He reached over and slammed the door closed, the sound making me jump. I stared at the floor again when I heard him sigh.

He walked to the stairs, pausing on the first step until I followed. He took my hand, leading, almost pulling me behind him. He let go when we reached the bedroom where again he slammed the door closed behind us.

"Strip," he said sternly.

My fingers fumbled with buttons and clasps, shaking so badly I was afraid I would never get anything off. Finally my clothes lay at my feet in a heap. I stood in the middle of the bedroom naked, eyes down, waiting for his next command.

But none came. The silence was so thick I wanted to look for him, fearing he had left the room and I hadn't heard him over the pounding of my heart in my ears. He knew me so well: as soon as I thought to turn my head, his hand snaked into my hair. He pulled firmly, tilting my head up to the ceiling. His tongue licked a line up my throat, his mouth moving to find my ear. He bit softly into my earlobe, his breath tickling the sensitive canal.

"Get on the bed, on your hands and knees," he growled against my ear. He put his hand to the small of my back to guide me, as if he were worried I would not do it. I had never disobeyed a direct order from him; I certainly wasn't going to start then.

I climbed as gracefully as I could onto the bed, took his desired pose, and waited. He had walked away, leaving me in that terrible silence again. It did not last long, though; minutes that felt like hours later I heard the familiar sound of the top dresser drawer opening. The grating of wood dowels against plastic grooves made my whole body break out into goose bumps. I could only stay there and hope that sound meant what I thought it did.

I was facing away from him, listening to the sound of his clothes hitting the floor behind me, of the drawer closing, of his feet on the wood floor as he walked back to me, but I still jumped when the first crack of the whip bit into my ass. I would be punished for this reaction later, I always was, but one punishment at a time. The second swat came harder, and I fought to stay up on my hands and knees. The third came just as hard, just as quick, leaving me gasping for breath and on the verge of begging for more.

I wouldn't do it, not yet anyway, because I knew he wanted me to react. He wanted to be able to use it against me later. He would whip my bared ass until I couldn't help but to cry out for him. He would do it harder and harder until I begged him for release.

He was a kind master. The best I had ever had. He would bring me to orgasm when I asked for it. He would bring me off over and over again until my body gave orgasms like gifts with every touch he bestowed upon me.

Then he would lay me over his knee and spank me with his bare hand as punishment for flinching at the whip, and for speaking out of turn by begging him to let me come.

It was my favorite game.

Tonight it wouldn't take long for the begging to begin. He hadn't used the whip on me in weeks. And that was my fault. I knew better than to ask him to use it on me. But I had asked him anyway, so he had hidden it away, threatening to never use it again.

I hadn't asked him for anything in weeks. I had been good. I had been so good. And when I heard that drawer open I almost cried in relief. I had missed it so much. I hadn't realized how much until the leather straps were biting into my ass again. I could feel welts rising up; it was torture not to cry out. But he was impatient tonight. He wanted his pound of flesh, and he wasn't going to take his time about getting it.

An hour from now I wouldn't be able to explain why I wanted this from him, why I needed it. I needed to feel the sharp sting of leather or wood or metal or anything, really, so long as it bit at my asscheeks. There was nothing more centering than to feel his love for me, and my trust of him, acted out as a smack to my bottom.

He flicked the whip one last time, one of the straps nicking my clit, and I begged. I begged him with tears choking my throat. I begged him to touch me, to fuck me, to let me come.

Every other time we had played this game he would roll me onto my back so I could feel the sheets rubbing against my tender ass while he fucked me. But tonight, he had other plans.

He left me lying facedown on the bed and raised my hips up while pushing down on my shoulders. He propped me up like I was a cat in heat, offering myself to him. He warned me not to come yet, then rammed two fingers inside of me. He worked his fingers over that sweet spot, the place I can never seem to find when fingering myself, twisting his hand so his knuckles scraped against it, pounding his hand against my clit until I cried out, unable to hold in the screams of my orgasm.

He removed his fingers and quickly replaced them with his cock. He slammed into me so hard I could feel his balls slapping against my clit. I rocked my hips into him, trying to meet his thrusts, but his hand tightened against my hip in silent warning. I came again when his hand connected with my ass. He spanked harder and harder while he fucked my drenched pussy. I could hear the wet slapping sounds he was making between my legs and I could barely stay up on my knees.

When he began to lose his rhythm I knew he was close. He dug his nails into the hot, tingling flesh on my bottom until we came together, both screaming, clawing, me the bedsheets and him my ass. He collapsed on my back, kissing the sweat off of my neck. I smiled into my pillow.

I had a new favorite game.

BLACK TULIPS

Kristina Lloyd

Nobody sucks cock like you do, baby," he said. "Nobody."

I was kneeling in front of him and he pinched my chin in his hand.

"Sheesh," he went on. "A schoolgirl in braces probably has more finesse."

His fingers were cruel but his words hurt more.

"I'm sorry," I replied. "It's not like I haven't been practicing."

"Exactly," he said. He bent close and cupped my face, his fingers on my cheeks squashing my lips into a rubbery figure eight. "So what's the fucking problem? Mouth getting tired, is it?" He gave my head a little shake, fingers still squeezing. "Jaw starting to ache?"

I grunted, trying to say no. In truth, my jaw *was* starting to ache, my neck too. The carpet was rough on my knees and my eyes stung with tears that sprang from being half-choked. But I didn't regard any of that as a drawback.

"What's that you say?" he asked. He tilted his ear at me and pressed more painfully on my cheeks, making it even trickier for me to talk. "Come on, speak up."

"No, I'm fine," I tried to say, except it sounded as if I were gargling with marbles.

"You know what really bugs me?" he said.

He released me with a small, dismissive push, then clasped his boner, idly pumping his fist. I stayed on my knees, mouth slack in case he wanted to push himself into me again.

"It's that thing you keep doing with your tongue," he said. "That licking, twirling thing. What the fuck is that?" The hand on his cock moved with the slowness of a threat, deliberate, heavy and measured. "Something you read in a magazine? A *technique* did they call it? Huh?"

There was nothing I could say so I just stayed there, waiting for the insults to come rolling in, gathering pace to debase me and crush me into my small, beautiful space. His words snaked through my thoughts like a filthy incantation and I gazed past him, my focus becoming loose, at a vase of blown tulips on the chest of drawers.

In the soft haze of a table lamp, their purplish black petals gleamed like velvet aubergines. Their heads drooped under the strain of fullness, gaps in the flowers displaying garish yellow stamens. Fallen petals lay scattered on the polished oak, decadent and wasted, and the tulip's exposed hearts were as stark as scars and wounds. On the edge of death, far removed from daylight and sunshine, the too-heavy flowers seemed artificial, sordid, and illicitly erotic. They made me think of hookers in fur coats loitering in seedy, neon-lit streets; of the lawless zones in cities where nobody notices they're under a rich black sky spangled with stars.

"Look at me," he said.

I did. In the dimness of the room, his eyes were shards of flint. "You think you know how to please me, don't you?" he went on. "Think a cute little blow job is going to make me happy. Well you ought to think again, missy, because I'm not happy, see? And if you don't shape up fast, I'm going to have to get myself another slut. Some whore who really knows how to work it."

I dropped my gaze to his cock, watching the leisurely slide of his fist and the fluidity of his wrist, his hand rolling with such easy movement. A violet-tinged flush suffused the head of his cock, bruise-dark and as sexy as the flowers.

"Look at me," he said again.

I raised my eyes to his.

"I'll throw you out onto the street," he said. "Because you're useless. I'll strip you naked first. Tie your ankles and wrists so you can't run away. Then I'll leave you on a corner, hang a sign around your neck saying 'World's worst cocksucker. Free to takers.' Is that what you want to happen?"

I shook my head. It was an effort to communicate. I could feel myself sinking, drowsy with lust, arousal pooling heavily in my cunt. I let his words carry me to another place, to another me who was far, far away. I was useless and worthless, no good at all. His insults made me uncomfortable and horny; and then I grew more uncomfortable because my horniness seemed wrong. Surely I should just be offended. Those swirling emotions had me feeling dislocated, dismantled, as if my sense of self were all at sea. When I start to slip and slide like that, I feel so permeable, wide open to anything and blissfully vulnerable.

"Now listen," he said. "I'm giving you one last chance. Suck my cock like I tell you and I might consider keeping you. Might not throw you out onto the streets. And, hey, if you're really good, who knows? I may even give you a reward. Now open your mouth again. Suck the head of my cock, just the head. Nice and slow and wet."

The wet part was difficult because my mouth was dry from me being on my knees, gaping in readiness. I swallowed hard then ran my tongue around my mouth, trying to find moisture in my cheeks and gums. Fastening my lips to his tip, I drew back and forth, lashing my tongue over his slippery end and its circlet of folded skin. After a while, I lightly fretted the taut thread on the underside, knowing how much he liked that.

"Good girl," he murmured, stroking my hair.

My groin fluttered in response. His tender approval sounded so sinister.

"Now go down, lips firm. That's right, all the way. Good girl. Now hold it there. Ho-old it."

I began to draw back, not yet ready for him.

"Hold!" he barked.

I couldn't. I spluttered around his shaft until he released me in a fit of coughing.

"Christ," he complained. "Let's try that again, shall we? Sink down a little, stretch your neck. Keep your throat open, okay? Now take me all the way."

I took him deep that time, focusing on relaxing and allowing him to glide into my throat. He groaned his pleasure and I bobbed on his tip, enjoying the feel of him butting beyond my tonsils and the way that made my mouth fill with moisture. It grew easier after that, hotter, wetter, and messier. I hoped I would pass his test, although not too soon because I wanted to savor the thrust of him in my throat, the way I could see nothing much but the blurred thatch of his pubes and pale pieces of skin.

I adore how cocksucking overtakes me, how it obscures my vision, robs me of speech, and fills my head, both the literal space of my mouth and the metaphorical space of my mind. I become a mere hole whose function is to be stuffed. I'm rendered inarticulate and all that I am, all my thoughts, memories, opinions, and hopes cease to matter. With his cock in my mouth, he and I are suspended in a moment of pure physicality.

He tangled his fingers in my hair, his hips lunging toward my face, cock pushing deep. "What do you think your reward's going to be? Huh?"

Obviously, I was in no position to answer but I knew exactly what my reward would be: getting fucked. He loosened his grip on my hair and I sucked back with tightly hugging lips. For several minutes, I glided up and down. I twirled my tongue around his shaft because, despite what he said, I knew he wanted this. Occasionally, I deep-throated him and every now and then, he'd get wild and challenge me to take him. He'd clasp my hair and show no mercy, fucking my face until it was clear I'd had enough.

"How much can you take?" he said. "How much cock?"

By the time he was done with me, I was exhausted, my body limp, my breath ragged, my cunt seeping. I sat back on my heels and was about to look up at him when movement caught my eye. I saw a cupped petal fall from one of the black tulips, quickly followed by another.

Of course, black flowers aren't black at all. It's an impossible color in nature but those tulips were as close to night as you could get. In the half-light, the petals had the sheen of plumage, a stormy, purplish underglow reminiscent of malevolent birds in a gothic fairy tale. But the bloated flowers were collapsing under the weight of their own dark beauty. The broken bouquet seemed to me a warning illustration of the obscenity of excess, of dissipation and of pleasure gone to seed. I found that both alluring and repellent.

"Give me your knickers," he said.

That, and a pair of knee-high socks, was all I was wearing.

I sat, pulled off my knickers, and handed them to him. He scrunched them into a ball.

"Open wide," he sang, merry as a dentist.

I obeyed and he crammed the ball into my mouth. His fingers were purposeful, pushing the fabric in deep, and his eyes were lit with sadistic glee. I bit down and breathed through my nostrils, resisting the urge to spit out the knickers. Then he tugged off my socks, slammed one lengthways across my lips and pulled tight.

"Won't be needing that hole for a while," he muttered as he knotted the sock at the back of my head. "Bend over."

I fell forward onto my hands and knees, huffing and puffing against the makeshift gag. He's resourceful, I'll grant him that. He likes to pervert everyday objects, snatching them up in a flash of inspiration or contemplating them with narrowed eyes and a wry smile. It's as if he takes over not only me but his environment, turning things to his advantage and using them for his own gain.

I heard him push down his clothes, felt him shuffle up behind me and place his hands on my buttocks. He pulled my cheeks wide and held me apart, making me squirm at the exposure. For several seconds, he did nothing and I could feel him looking at the valley of my arse and the hanging folds of my cunt. He brushed his cock up and down, tormenting me with his nearness before finally plunging into my warm, wet center. I groaned loudly, his thickness sending pleasure rippling through my body, and I kept on grunting, my noises muffled by the gag, as he pounded away.

When he'd tired of me that way, he had me lie sideways on the floor, my knees tucked up. He managed to stay inside me, twisting his body to fit our new angle.

"Hot little slut," he gasped. "Likes getting fucked. This way, that way, any way."

He drove in and out, his thigh bumping against my puffed-up clit, taking me closer and closer to the edge.

"You gonna come?" he asked.

I nodded, whimpering into the fabric gag. He kept right on going, thigh nudging so perfectly until I was there, poised at my peak. I came hard, collapsing like those swollen tulips, my orgasm tumbling through me. He drove harder still. I felt weak as a kitten. Inside I was sensitive and pulpy, my pinkness clinging to the thrust of his cock. He came on a groan of triumph, buried balls-deep inside me, and then we held the position, catching our breath as our bodies softened.

Except for the lift of our shoulders the room was perfectly still. Then another plum black petal dropped from the tulips. It landed gently on the furred heap on the polished surface. In the lamplight, the petals glowed darkly, dustings of yellow pollen staining their bases like a squandered drug.

He rubbed my buttocks, his hand slow and soothing. Printing a kiss on my neck, he withdrew. He removed my underwear gag, and I ran my tongue around my dry mouth. I smiled at him and he smiled back, eyes full of kindness and love.

"You okay?" he asked, brushing a wisp of hair from my face.

I nodded. "You?"

We always ask this as we tiptoe from the darkness to the light. *You okay?*

He's nasty and mean to me because I like it and so does he. But it's an impossible thing. It doesn't last. It's base and beautiful for a moment in time. And then we move away, drifting back to where we live in daylight and sunshine but always ready to fall into our shadows.

MR. SMITH, MS. JONES WILL SEE YOU NOW

Malcolm Harris

Marge, I'm going to be staying in the City tonight. I've got a meeting with an out-of-town client and it's gonna go late…. No, honey, don't worry about me. I've made reservations at Antonelli's. Yes, that's right. You just enjoy your evening alone. I'm sure it'll be a welcome break from farting and football….Yeah, yeah, I know, but I'm sure you'll enjoy the solitude anyway. I'll see you tomorrow evening and we'll have the whole weekend to lounge around together. Maybe go see a movie. I love you, too, sweetheart."

I close the cell and my eyes are drawn surreptitiously to the receptionist. She stares at me and smiles. Actually, it isn't so much a smile as a smirk. The intercom on her desk beeps and she picks up the handset.

"Yes?" She pauses, listening to someone on the other end, and looks at me again. She continues to smirk as she runs a hand over her breast and gives it a squeeze, ending in a nipple tweak. She laughs. "All right," she says, and hangs up the phone.

"Mr.—" she pauses, "Smith?" There is an underlying hint of honeyed contempt. "Ms. Jones will see you now." She licks her upper lip and searches for smudges on her clawlike, neon purple nails. Never looking up again she says, "I believe you know the way." She pushes a button on her desk and the door lock buzzes.

I walk through the door and hear it close behind me. It feels like going through an air lock; it's almost like being weightless, crossing that barrier. There is no sound in the hallway at all. I was scared the first time I came here, having no idea what to expect. Now, I can feel the tension drain away with each step. I'd like to come here every week, but I make sure I get here at least once a month; I need it now, to stay sane.

There are four doors on each side of this hallway and every time I come, I wonder what's behind them. I don't suppose it matters because my door is at the end. There won't be any other doors for me, unless She says so.

I can't believe it took me fifty-five years. What a fucking waste. Well, I suppose it wasn't really fifty-five years. After all, I couldn't have discovered sexual satisfaction at the age of one or ten, but wouldn't it have been nice to find this before I became a paunchy, balding, out-of-shape man of fifty-five?

She will get me into shape again.

She's probably the only person who could.

At the door, I knock twice and wait for admittance.

Once inside, I close the door behind me and turn toward Ms. Jones. She says, "You'll find your things over there," and points a beautifully manicured finger at the floor in the corner of the room. "I'm very busy today and really should be doing other things, so don't waste my time."

I catch a glimpse of her before sinking to my hands and knees. It will be a good night. She's wearing her tight black rubber corset: the one that comes up to just below her breasts. I want to run my hands down her sides to feel her delicate frame encased in that shiny, black covering. I spend a lot of time imagining what it would feel like, as I'm never allowed that particular sensation.

Her hands and arms are bare right now. It shows off the deep red of her short nails. She wears black stockings, held up by garters attached to her corset, and her black calfskin boots, perhaps my favorites. Although they don't have spiked heels to torment me, the leather's so soft, and they transmit the heat of her skin so readily to my hands and lips. They're completely flat, with smooth, unmarked, leather soles, really more like slippers. They encase her legs and rise just past her knees. Sometimes, she lets me stroke her legs through the boots, when I worship her.

Did I see her dark-haired pussy peeking out from under the corset? I can't be sure. She doesn't allow me the luxury of lingering eyes. I catch all this in a split second, before casting my eyes down. I keep them on the floor until she tells me otherwise.

In that split second, my cock has detected all it needs. It's painfully pressed against my zipper, with only a thin layer of silk between. It's not like I can get this hard in a flash, I'm not saying that. No, the blood starts flowing as soon as I hear the door buzzer: a true Pavlovian response. By the time I get to the inner sanctum and see Her, it's all over. Nothing gets me hard like Ms. Jones. It's like I'm seventeen again, but with the control of age and experience.

I was always drawn to the strict teachers in school or the nurses and hygienists who had a cold, no-nonsense air about them, but I never realized why. My wife, Margie, is the sweetest, most loving, and gentle woman I've ever known. She worships me and does everything she can to make my life easier.

I had a talk with her once about my need for dominance, and she understood. She even tried accommodating me. But she couldn't give me what I needed. The situation made her laugh, and she found role-playing too embarrassing. The dominance just isn't in her. Even if she could pull off a scenario, it would be total make-believe and I'd know. Make-believe doesn't cut it. I need the real thing.

I crawl to the corner and quickly begin removing my clothes.

"What's that?" she says, when I get my pants off. She walks over to me, carrying a thin bamboo cane in her hand. She runs it up and down the underside of my cock. "Some boys are simply incorrigible, aren't they?"

"Yes, Ma'am."

"Hurry up with those clothes and get ready. I haven't got all night."

"Yes, Ma'am." Quickly, I remove the rest of my clothes and put on the locking, heavy leather ankle and wrist cuffs she's provided. They feel so right against my skin. Is it hot in here? I'm naked; you'd think I'd be cold, but I notice a light sheen of perspiration has begun to form under my arms and on my upper lip. My balls stretch out and hang slightly lower.

My wife, my little Margie, did this for me. That's how much she loves me. She was the one who found Ms. Jones and made an appointment. It was my fifty-fifth birthday present. Can you believe it? And she didn't tell me what the appointment was for; she just told me I had an appointment with a Ms. Jones, at this address after work, as my birthday present. Someone should have taken pictures of my reaction—birthday cake, twenty-nine ninety-five, appointment with a dominatrix, priceless!

"All right, stand up."

Ms. Jones uses her cane under my cock to help me up. Once I'm standing, she gives my rear end a quick, playful swat with it. I feel the burn, as the line forms.

"It's time for your collar. If there are no objections…"

"No, Ma'am." Why on earth would I have any objections? But she always asks me. I feel it go round my neck and her cool fingers fasten the buckle and click the padlock closed in back. I sense the first drop of precome drip from the end of my cock as she takes a dog leash from a hook at her waist and attaches it to a ring on the front of the collar. She drops it and it bounces off my chest and hangs loose, down past my cock. The metal chain links are cold.

"Sit on your stool and put your knee pads on. I won't have you complaining halfway through the session that your arthritis is killing you." She turns and walks away.

She's left a pair of heavy leather knee pads for me. The insides are soft thick foam, which conforms to my knees. Without these, I'd never be able to hold up.

I always feel invincible in here with Ms. Jones, but there are some things about age that are completely unforgiving. I hear her turn and walk away.

When I got home, that first night, I thanked Margie profusely and we made love with more passion than we'd been able to summon in years. I never mention it, but I know Margie knows I still come here. I think she's glad but she doesn't talk about it, so neither do I.

"If you're quite through, come over here."

I quickly drop to my hands and knees and crawl across the room to Ms. Jones's chair. The leash trails between my legs as I crawl. When I reach her, she uses it to pull me into a sitting position.

"What do you think you're looking at?"

I drop my eyes. She's in a high, wooden chair, on a dais. Staring straight ahead, I see I was right; she isn't wearing any panties. I am given a lovely view of her pussy, spread slightly open. Thick, curly, black hair frames the almost purple interior.

Her clit is prominently displayed at the top of her slit. Does she like me, or is it the thought of the games she will play that arouses her?

"I know how much you like that view. You'll get a better one later," she says as a petite, leather-clad foot fills my vision.

She presses the sole of her boot to my lips and I kiss it, reverently.

"Lick it. Lick it completely clean, and don't forget the heel."

As I bathe it with my tongue, she pulls the leash to her, keeping my face held tightly against her foot. Once she's satisfied, she tells me to stop, and she rubs the damp leather over my eyes, my cheeks, my mouth, and chin. She loosens her hold on the leash and pushes against my face with her boot as she rises, pushing me down to the floor.

"On your back," she says. Her voice has a musical, commanding tone I can't get enough of. It really doesn't matter what she says to me, it's that sound; it always sends chills down my spine, directly to my balls.

When I'm lying on my back, she uses the foot I've cleaned to rub against my nipples, making them hard. She slides her foot lower and presses against my stomach.

"Are you working out, like I told you? This is not transforming quickly enough. I can see that I'll have to look over your diet again and modify it even more. I'll not have you dying of a heart attack because you have no control over your lifestyle!" She prods my flab. "Do you want to make that charming wife of yours a widow? All this has to go—or you will."

"I'm sorry, Ms. Jones. I'll do better."

"Who told you to talk? Did I ask you a question?"

"No, Ma'am."

"That's right," she says, giving my gut one last toe prod. She slides her foot lower and tweaks my cock with the toe. She moves her foot between my legs and prods my balls, then brings it up to mash my erection against my groin.

I must have moaned, because she stops and says, "What's that, boy?" I don't say anything and she goes back to grinding my genitals. "Good boy," she says, and I melt.

Eventually, she forces her foot between my legs and slightly under my bottom. She pulls me to a sitting position with the leash and I find myself astride her foot. It is small enough to almost completely fit inside my asscrack. The soft leather feels amazing and I rock from side to side on it, forcing it further up my crack.

"Stop that."

"Yes, Ma'am."

"Wiggling like that is lewd. I won't stand for that type of behavior. Stand up. Bend over and put your hands on the seat of my chair."

Placing my hands on the chair, I notice she's taken the cover off the seat, exposing the opening. Anticipation of what's to come makes my cock jump just as I feel the cane stroke. I get five hard ones, but I can barely focus on the pain for thoughts of her perfect pussy over my face.

She pulls the leash, breaking me out of my thoughts, and traces the marks on my ass with her finger. "Very nice." She worries one particular welt with a fingernail. "Put your head in the headrest."

Down on the floor, I place my head in a sling directly under the opening in the seat of her chair, and put my arms down by my sides. I feel her clip my wrists to eyebolts on the legs of the chair and then wrap the leash around both my cock and balls. She brings it up between my balls, separating them, and then wraps it around the whole package once more, pulling it tight.

"Put those feet flat on the floor."

I bend my knees and do as I'm told. She spreads my legs apart.

"I want these legs spread as far as possible. What are you waiting for?"

I spread my feet until my hamstrings ache and she fastens my ankle cuffs to other eyebolts, keeping my legs in position. She sits down, confining my vision to only a few square inches of pussy. I breathe her musk in deeply through my nose.

"Now that's a nice view," she says. "And good access, too."

The cane slides between my asscheeks and soon I feel the tip resting on my asshole.

"I better not see those knees begin to close. What are you waiting for? Lick!"

I wallow in the taste and scent of her. I really had very little experience providing good cunnilingus before Ms. Jones taught me how to perform it properly. It takes a while, but it's worth the extra effort. I tongue, suck, and lick for a good twenty minutes or more. It takes a while for the first orgasm, but the second follows fairly quickly.

It took exercise and practice to be able to continue for this length of time. There were some sessions spent entirely on oral exercises and cunnilingus, but it was worth it. Margie has definitely benefited from all the hard work.

Ms. Jones smacks me between the legs with her cane, hitting the underside of my ass and my inner thighs. I know this is just a warm-up for things to come and my imagination runs wild. There are so many things she could do—has done with me. Her knowledge supersedes my ability to even imagine. I should probably be punished for these kinds of thoughts. An endless stream of precome dribbles from my cock...and I have miles to go before I sleep.

KING OF
THE ROAD

Bella Dean

My god, what is it?"

"A motorcycle."

"I can see that. But why? Why did you buy me a motor-cycle?"

"You'll look hot on a motorcycle."

Chad was grinning. It wasn't his normal grin or his happy grin. It was the kind of grin that made my belly tighten and my neck prickle and yes, made my pussy wet. "Oh, no."

That was all I said because I knew by that grin and the very odd and unexpected gift of a motorcycle that this would not be good, could not be good. It would be bad and probably embar-rassing or scary. But then I pressed my knees together at the growing heat between my legs. Because after the bad, would come the good. And Chad's version of good could be fucking heaven if you were brave enough.

"Oh, yes. Yes, yes, yes, my little buxom bombshell. This will be fan-fucking-tastic." he laughed softly and that laugh raised the hairs on my arms. I studied his dark eyes and felt twin spots of color rise on my cheeks. It felt as if I had been smacked—hard.

"What are you going to make me do, baby?" God help me, the "baby" came out in a pleading tone: begging; wheedling; desperate.

He pulled me to him and I let him. I burrowed against him and he stroked my hair. "It's okay, babe. We'll get thought this. Little steps. One at a time. It will be fine." He said it all as if he would have nothing to do with the outcome, as if he wasn't the puppet master of the whole thing.

"Okay," I said. I would trust him.

He kissed me and I let him. And when he pushed me back against the pegboard wall and lifted my skirt, I let him. And when he parted my thighs and opened me wide, I let him fuck me.

"We have this and this. Oh, and these. And this. There. That should do it. Smoking hot." He grinned and my belly fluttered.

Excitement, fear, want, terror: all of it shooting through me, coiled under my skin like a glowing white light. "Oh, my god. I don't know." I held up the dress. "Dress" was stretching it: scrap was more like it. It was Dominatrix meets Gidget, short and black and flippy, but with a whip. Gidget with a whip, that was it. "Jesus. I can't pull this off."

"Sure you can. And then I'll pull it off. You can do this and then we'll move on to the next."

I swallowed hard and held the dress in front of my curvy frame. I'm no freaking pencil. I'm what Chad calls pinup shaped, which is fine. Bouncy boobs, bouncy blonde hair, heart-shaped mouth, big blue eyes—I played them up. But this…this… nondress: I would feel naked, speeding down the street on a motorcycle in the equivalent of a skirted bathing suit, starlet gloves, and jaunty hat. Maybe some other woman could pull it off, but not me, no fucking way.

"I can't," I squeaked and dropped the mess of black sex-kitten clothes at his feet. Then I stepped back and held my breath. This would not be good.

When Chad is angry or disappointed or challenged, his face changes. From handsome, lean, easy smiling Chad to cut, chiseled jaw clenched tight Chad. Both are sexy as hell. One makes my nipples hard and my heart skip erratically. He turned big dark eyes to me and said softly. "Oh, you can and you will. Now take the jeans off. Tank top, too. You have to take a ride."

I almost talked back. Almost is the key word. I knew there was a reason for all this. And when it came to our bedroom games and the things that led up to them, Chad is king, master, and commander, the head honcho. I took one look at his eyes and then he licked his lips, probably not intentionally, but the flash of pale pink tongue over full bottom lip reminded me of all the things that tongue could achieve, and how generous Chad could be with me when he was pleased.

I dropped my jeans.

I blinked and I was in hell, standing in the driveway in the blazing sun in front of my motorcycle: *my motorcycle.* I shifted from foot to foot like I had to pee. Honestly, I did. And I knew the vibration of the bike under me would do very little to help. "Climb up on your bike now, baby. I'll be the guy behind you in the convertible. Watching your ass and watching the other guys watch your ass."

I turned to beg him. *Oh, please, oh, please, I changed my mind. Don't make me. I'll look like a fool. I'll look ridiculous. I am not the woman who can do this.* He read my look, swatted my ass hard enough to steal my breath, and growled. "Get. On. The. Bike."

I did as I was told, mostly because that one hard smack had sent a blissful and swift contraction of want between my legs. This bike would be the death of me. I closed my eyes, my heart an erratic drumbeat under my breast, and thanked my lucky stars that my brother Bobby had forced me to learn to ride his bike when we were teenagers. I gunned her and the motorcycle vibrated to life under me.

"Just down Heins and back should be fine. Go for it."

I could barely hear him above the rumble and growl but I nodded and took off out of the driveway; not too fast, not too slow. At first I was terrified. The wind whipped my hair despite the hat. The sun burned the long black gloves; they soaked up the heat of the day like banked coals. I would not have been surprised had my arms burst into flames. And the wind; well, the fucking wind was worse than a lecherous man, lifting my dress and displaying the very teeny tiny black thong that Chad had put me in. An eye patch, that is what my panties looked like.

I quickly encountered wolf whistles, car horns, yells, and a few cross women shouting that I should be ashamed. But the sun was on my back and the MG driven by Chad was behind me, right on my tail, so to speak. I tilted my head back as I rounded the curve and felt the breeze on my barely covered breasts noticing how much cooler the air was when I was in motion.

"Hey, baby, love the pantiiiiiiiiiiies!"

A van rocketed past and I could practically feel Chad taking it in: me on the bike, the power I had and portrayed, and the power he had over me just coming up in the rear. I couldn't help it. I started singing "King of the Road" at the top of my lungs. I yelped and then laughed when I heard Chad tap the horn. "Faster, baby, faster!" he bellowed and I opened her up.

We were up and back Heins Road way too fast for me.

As the garage door made its noisy descent, Chad was cutting the hot little dress off of me with work shears. When the door settled against the stained concrete floor, he was peeling off my gloves. The hat ended up on a peg on the board and the boots, well, the boots stayed. Bent over the tool bench, ass in the air, his thick fingers deep in my pussy, I came the first time.

"And you said you couldn't do it," he growled, sinking his cock deep inside of me. I gripped the vise on the workbench. The MG's engine popped and ticked as it cooled. Chad yanked me back hard, buried in me, and only the toes of my boots were touching the floor as he fucked me.

"I liked it." I had to tell the truth. At first I had been terrified, but in the end I had liked it. I put my head against the coarse table, gripped the vise, listened to my hair whisper over the wood.

"You looked fucking hot, baby. Every guy out there nearly crashed his car. And the women. Damn. The women were pissed. Except for the ones who wanted to get right where I am. Right between these sweet thighs."

The pressure in my pussy was unbearable, and the more he talked the tighter I got. The bike had stimulated everything. I had to pee, I had to come, I was tight, I was soft. It was all mixed up and I could feel the phantom vibration in my pussy, in my ass. He shoved into me and I felt all of that release and I came again, came hard and fast with just my toes touching earth.

Chad leaned in and licked my neck, letting his own orgasm take over. Then his voice rolled in my ear like smoke. "Tomorrow we move on."

Fear skittered down my spine and another spasm erupted in my cunt.

* * *

"Are you fucking kidding me?" I waved the new gear at him. Let him get mad. Let him get that look on his face. He was insane. Insane! There was no way I could do this.

"Get dressed."

That look flashed over him and the tone in his voice made me cringe and purr all at once. I shoved down my shorts and ripped off my tank, furious, livid. I stepped into the black spandex hot pants, pulled on the bra bikini top, and shoved the hat on my head. Today I had fingerless black riding gloves. And a big-ass lightning bolt necklace. I moved and my right tit popped out of the top.

"No."

"Yes. Get on the bike. Now."

"I'll lose my top the first bump I go over," I yelped, but I marched on my tall black boots. I admit, there was a little more sway in my ass today. I was starting to like my bike and what it did for me "down there."

"That's the point. You look hot." This time, he licked my lower lip and I let him. He bit me and I let him. He shoved his big hand down the front of my pants in the driveway and I let him. He slid his fingers deep inside of me, curled them perfectly a few times and just like that, I was riding on the edge of coming. "Now get on the bike."

"Yes, majesty," I only half joked.

"That's more like it," he said and smacked my ass once—hard; harder than hard; painfully hard.

I climbed on and gunned it. This time I ripped out of the driveway, the MG right behind me.

More catcalls, more whistles, more words, but fuck that: more power. I let her open up and really took the hills. The bike vibrated under me and through me, sending power and adrenaline and a bit of fear and lots of arousal. I wanted to be bent over this damn bike and fucked senseless. I wanted to sprawl across it and suck Chad's cock. I wanted to have him ride behind me and reach around and get me off as we crested a hill or hit a dip. I wanted a lot when I rode the bike.

I hit a bump and my breasts bounced out from behind the teeny tiny black triangles of fabric that made up my top. I let them be. The sun felt good on my nipples and the wind teased them to perfect pink peaks. A car drove by, and the man stared, grinning, his mouth wide open, his eyes wide; his wife looking pissed.

I tossed my head back and laughed, gave her more gas, and reached the top of Heins. It was time to turn around; too bad. As I turned, going past Chad, he yelled, "I'm going to fuck you till you can't talk when we get home."

I left a lot of open mouths and wide eyes in my wake but I was more intent on the vibration through my pussy, and how wet I was, how much I wanted Chad, and how free I felt. I barely got the bike in the garage before he came up behind me, dipped, caught me up on his shoulder, and draped my belly across the bike seat.

Hot metal, leather, oil filled my head and he knelt behind me, wrenching my thighs wide, and attacking me with his tongue. He traced my nether lips, sucking me in, licked me until I was begging. Then he came around and bared his cock for me, something I can rarely resist.

I gripped the warm, well-worn seat and took him in between my lips. I loved the taste of him on my tongue, how warm he was; how smooth but hard his cock was, such a paradox of flesh. "Fuck me, Chad. Baby. I'm dying."

And it was true. I only had to ask once. I had been a good listener. He even told me. "You're a good girl, Don. A good little soldier. You should see your ass on that bike. And the way your breasts bounce around. Hair blowing in the wind. A sweet little ride. You. And the bike." Then he was balls deep in me and I was draped over the bike, legs splayed, a hot little motorcycle whore.

As I came, I wondered what tomorrow would bring. Excitement and fear warred in my belly, but my pussy won because I came again.

My final trip down Heins was made topless. I kicked and pouted and screamed. Topless. Top-Less. A pair of black bikini bottoms and boots. No gloves or hat, even!

"I'll get arrested."

"I'll come bail you out." He pushed my bare legs into the panties and pulled them up over my ass. "Go."

I started to cry. Deep down I knew it would do no good, but I cried. "People will see."

"Which is the point."

"I'm not that woman. I can't pull it off."

"Oh, baby. You will break hearts, trust me."

"They'll laugh."

"They'll want to fuck you."

"They'll want to fuck me!" I wailed. A very real trail of tears streaked my face.

"Good. I want them to want to fuck you. And then I'll fuck you."

"Chad!"

"Get on the fucking bike. Now. No more."

I got on the bike. I started her up. A breeze blew over my breasts, a cool kiss of air that was like a thousand gentle tongues, and I actually moaned. I put the kickstand up and started down the drive. "Donna!" I stopped. Chad got on behind me and put his arms around my waist. "Now go."

"Oh, shit."

"You got it." He put his teeth against my shoulder and I drove.

We passed a van with four men in it. All eyes were on me, and I felt the thrill of it in my cunt. When we cleared them and were the only ones on the black ribbon of road, Chad pinched my clit through my panties. I sobbed. A sports car shot by in a blare of shouts and horns. Chad edged closer so I could feel his cock against my asscrack. He pinched my clit again and I bit my tongue. I was going to come. Another motorcycle passed and I prayed the driver wouldn't go off the road. Chad rubbed a hard hot circle through the fabric. I was one inch closer. The bike vibrated right up through the core of me. Wind ripped at my hair and I was thankful for the big black sunglasses I had been allowed. Chad cupped my breasts on a clear stretch of road, pinched my nipples, returned to my clit.

"Oh, god." He couldn't hear me. The wind stole my voice, tore it from the air in front of me, flung it away.

The vibration snaked through my pelvis. Chad rubbed circles, sneaky and lazy. We crested a hill and when we shot down the other side, my belly dropped like I was on a roller coaster and my orgasm vibrated under my skin. It felt like heaven. It smelled like oil. It tasted like cool wind. It sounded like Chad in my ear humming, "King of the Road."

CALLING DAVID HASSELHOFF

Jax Baynard

I became a Dominatrix because of the clothing, although the word *clothing* is a fairy euphemistic one to describe what I wear when I am working. Even at the office, there was always the joke about my "dominatrix shoes," which tended to be black, strappy, and shiny, and whenever I dressed up I wore tight little black dresses.

Eventually the shoes got bigger and the dresses got smaller, until there was no reasonable way to appear in public wearing them, and I was shopping at stores that do not advertise in the *Yellow Pages* and do not have outlets at the mall. I was basically prancing around my apartment at night with the shades drawn, turning myself on, but no one else—which, frankly, seemed a shame. That stuff is expensive.

I finally got into the business through a friend of a friend who could tell I was interested to the point of obsession. She hooked me up with someone named Lady Jane (not her real name) who was happy to help me familiarize myself with how things worked in the world of S/M. She is very sweet, Lady Jane, and only dominant in the sense that she most often plays mothers to men who want to be infants. There are more of them out there than you might think. She bottle-feeds them and changes their diapers and croons lullabies to them—and she gets paid money like you wouldn't believe.

My first actual job was on a rainy weekend when Jane called to ask me if I could take a client for her. "You know the gig," she said. "It's not complicated." I felt a little spiral of excitement in my belly, and I asked her if I could do a variation on the theme.

There was a long pause. I think she had a fever of about 104 at the time. The she said weakly, "Whatever turns you on, honey." She says "honey" in such a maternal way. So I went as Dommy Mommy, in a black push-up bra with metal studs and a black leather apron. And when Teddy was a bad boy, I spanked him. And the more he cried, the harder I spanked him. It was a lot of fun. When Lady Jane got better, he went back to her, but sometimes when he's been a really bad boy, he comes to see me.

It didn't take long to get established. Almost everyone was friendly and helpful because there is more than enough work to go around. And I kept my day job, so I only work nights and weekends. My niche is whips. I do pain, but I don't like blood, and I won't push anyone past his limit. I always give my clients the same safeword: *David Hasselhoff*. Anyone who knows me knows he can just sing out, and I'll stop immediately and we'll take a break. I'm pretty relaxed, I guess, for a Dom. I just like to pretend I'm at the rodeo with my favorite whip—a plaited rawhide bullwhip from Argentina. I keep her oiled and beautiful, and I just want you to know that while I have thought about sleeping with her, I never have.

Thompson turned up during a record-breaking summer heat wave, and all I remember about his first three months as a client was how sweaty everything was. Thompson is one of my favorites: he's low maintenance. He just wants to be beaten, sometimes in different ways, but always hard, and he never makes a fuss about my rates. He's not game-y. He doesn't care about the psychology, which is what drives most people. He's about as straightforward as they come.

That is except for one Sunday afternoon. He arrived late, rumpled and grumpy, which is not like him at all. He gave me a slitty-eyed stare, which turned speculative, then plopped himself down on my couch and announced that he wanted to try something different.

I stroked my whip and said, "How different?"

In retrospect, I think he might have been having a crisis. I don't know much about him personally. That's the point. I'm not part of their regular lives. His answer caught me flat-footed with surprise in five-inch heels.

"I want you to take off all that gear, and I want to touch you all over and put my face in your cunt."

Then he stared at me in a manner that I can only categorize as challenging. I'm very female, but not feminine. I have long legs and a killer ass and no waist to speak of. My breasts aren't that great, which doesn't really matter because there's so much you can do with them. I like to glue black vinyl spiderwebs over them. The nipple is the center of the web, and I black that out with lipstick you can get at any goth beauty supply. I can make it look like I have a waist by tightening a few straps here and there, but I have as many insecurities as the next woman. What I'm saying is that I wasn't sure I wanted to be girl-naked with Thompson.

Don't challenge a Dom, though. You might not like the results.

"All right," I agreed, beginning the long process of unbuckling my thigh-high black patent-leather boots. "You can do all that to me, but you have to let me do something to you in return."

He had crossed his arms over his chest and was looking a little insolent. When he raised his eyebrows, I said, "You have to let me fuck you with a strap-on." The eyebrows stayed up, but the insolence was gone. We had never talked about it. I just tossed the concept out there on a whim. Straight, gay, or bi, I believe about 90 percent of men want to take it up the ass at least once, just to see what it feels like—which, from what I can tell, seems pretty damn good. Still, I was surprised when he said yes. I was sure he'd say no; now my out was gone, too.

Thompson is an attractive man if you go in for that sort of thing. Tall, blond, rangy, heterosexual, he's at the top of the heap in a patriarchal society. We rolled around on the carpet for a while. He put his hands all over me and his face in my cunt, as promised, and to be honest, I was starting to enjoy it. So I moved all my sexual energy to the heel of my right foot and held it there. When his time was up, I tied him to the bed and strapped one on. He looked a little apprehensive, so I reminded him that the safeword would still work, despite our deal.

Before I lubed up, I licked around his anus for a while, until he was squirming and pushing himself into the mattress, and then I toyed with his balls and cock to keep him occupied while I started in. I had one greedy moment when I wished it was my cock—that it was real so I could feel everything, but I wouldn't give up my clit for anything in the world, so I let the fantasy go. I kept up a nice, steady rhythm, thrusting in his ass and stroking his cock. Fast, but not too fast. When he began to moan and jerk his hips, I increased the pace a little. In regular sex, it's a free-for-all. Everybody comes and they're happy. Or nobody comes and nobody's happy. Or one comes and the other sulks. It's a mixed bag. But if it's your job and you're professional and you're good at it, there's some skill involved. I judged the timing perfectly, stopping cold right before he was about to come. I kept hold of his dick, but low at the base, and I wouldn't let him move. I put my lips to his ear, asked, "Do you want to come now?" and got the obvious answer.

"Say my name," I demanded.

"Jax!" he gasped.

That's my Dom name that everyone knows.

"Say my *girl-name*," I insisted. "I won't let you come until you say it."

Poor man. I'd only told him once, a long time ago. I moved back a little, as if I was going to pull out.

He moaned. "*Rachel*," he bit out.

"Oh, good boy," I said approvingly. I surged forward, pushing the dildo in as far as it would go, then a tiny bit farther. I gave his cock a hard jerk, and pushed my thumb up, pressing it into the sensitive spot where the crown meets the shaft. He convulsed, coming and coming like a dam bursting, until even I was impressed. Afterward, he lay there red-faced, struggling to catch his breath. He said, "That was…" a few times, then gave up. I could tell by his face that he was searching for a superlative; he just didn't have enough blood in his brain to find one.

"Glad you liked it," I said tartly. "Maybe you'll think about it the next time you want to break my rules."

"I didn't have to call for David Hasselhoff," he responded, and I had to bite down on the smile that threatened to escape.

GHOSTS OF THE WILDFLOWER

Thomas S. Roche

'll call her Jill; I'll call it the Wildflower Inn; I'll refer to it as
Xtown, and I won't disclose the state. The Pacific Northwest is
a big damn place, so search if you so desire; the ghosts of Wildflower sleep sweet and undisturbed, and I don't wish to encourage
disturbing them, crazy as it may sound. If I am violating their trust
by sharing this story, then it's no greater a violation than the one
I give to Jill, whom I trussed like a turkey and tied facedown, ass-
up, to a four-poster bed, and may have had a threesome or a four-
some or possibly a fivesome with. It seemed kind of crowded on
that cheap motel bed. Or maybe she was just fucking with me.

Jill had a lithe frame and pale skin and coal black hair, or
more accurately, Revlon Blue Black #1. I loved to put her in
bondage not only because she so adored it, but because she was
a consummate exhibitionist and loved having her picture taken.
We had a sexual relationship that careened between explosive-
ness and disinterest, with rope and leather being the usual ingre-
dients that ignited the former.

Perhaps more pertinent to this story, Jill was so far past being a Smart-Assed Masochist that no sane bondage top would have bothered with her without a ball gag close at hand. She loved to fuck with people, and I don't even know if she always understood that she was doing it. The second the clothes came off, she would utter a stream of dirty talk in singsong, making the filthiest utterances sound like ironic ridicule.

She wasn't evil, she was just drawn that way.

But outside the bedroom, not in bondage? No singsong at all; Jill was all straight-faced irony and verbal sparring, tossing sarcasm into casual conversation and engaging in conversational hoaxes to rival Clifford Irving. She would spew stories of her improbably weird origins and unlikely adventures, never cracking a smile even after she'd admitted to fucking with you. It might be a story about where she grew up, her sexual past, her financial dealings, or her BDSM interests. She claimed to be a diagnosed compulsive liar, and would say "Listen very closely, now: Everything I say is a lie. I. Am. Lying," with a completely straight face and seemed to hope that someday someone, on hearing that, would scream "Does not compute!" in a robotic voice and start spewing smoke.

This was eventually how I could tell Jill was sexually aroused: she started sounding sarcastic, rather than deadpan. There were two speeds to this woman: Alanis Morissette and Wednesday Addams.

She never seemed to work, never had much money, but always had some pocket cash, which would have made me think she was some sort of criminal if she didn't keep telling me she was. "No, really, I'm in the mafia, they allow girls now," she'd say so convincingly that some small part of me wanted to believe it, and more gullible members of our social circle would buy it hook, line, and sinker.

Once exposed as a charlatan on any particular point—which saint was used in the "making" ceremony, for instance—she would "tell the truth," which would usually be something even less likely.

In case you ever happen to meet this woman, I'll break the news to you right now: not only was she not in the mafia; she was also never an agent for MI-6. I don't think.

In any event, Jill's habit of confabulation made her astonishingly entertaining company on long drives, and her habit of loving perverted sexual bondage, coupled with her flexible frame, made her astonishingly entertaining company in cheap motels once those long drives were over. We ended up taking a road trip together during a period when I was unemployed. "Don't you have a job or something?" I asked her. "Not this week," she said.

Our destination was nowhere in particular; we drove languidly through the Pacific Northwest for a few days in my beat-up Volkswagen, and had weird sex near Reno, strange encounters outside of Boise, and perverse goings-on at a rest stop. But the strangest encounter we had was in this place I'll call Xtown.

It was not yet the time of year to be comfortably wandering around the Northwest, and we'd had a hellish experience the night before with the rank stink of a dairy farm permeating a hotel room without heat. It was our fifth day away from home. We were getting ready to start back the next morning. We decided to stay at what I'll call the Wildflower Inn—a glorified motel that called itself a B&B. It had a web page that promised four-poster beds, to which Jill said, "Hot," and I had to agree. I grunted about the price, and "I'll put it on my card," she said, her first disclosure that she actually possessed a credit card.

I let her check in while I waited in the car listening to

Bauhaus on MP3. She came laughing out of the office and held up a totally old-school key, with a diamond-shaped key chain, emerald green, with the room number on white. "The old lady at the desk says this room is haunted," Jill told me.

I didn't even bother to say, "Bullshit."

"She had some weird story about a trucker whose wife murdered him in this very room. The old lady wouldn't say any more, but it sounds like it involved a hooker."

"And crystal meth?"

"Around here that goes without saying."

I still didn't bother to say, "Bullshit," but she had me wondering: you meet some complete and total lunatics in the Heartland of this great America, so I couldn't say for certain that Jill hadn't heard some freaky story from some skanked-out old lady in the office of a cheap motel. What I could say for certain, was that I had one night left to put the room's four-poster bed to use, and I looked forward to tying Jill up.

"Four-poster bed" was a vast and terrifying understatement, but the stupid thing did have bedposts, and the room was warm, almost uncomfortably so.

As soon as the door closed I shot the deadbolt with bondage-obsessed finality and got Jill up against the wall, holding her wrists far above her and thrusting my hand under her shirt.

She squirmed. "Let me take a shower first," she whined. "I'm filthy."

"Yes you are," I said, spinning her around. Her shirt was still pulled up and I slapped her perfect tits as I pulled her wrists behind her. I pinned them in the small of her back and reached around to get her pants open.

She was normally not this obedient, but I could tell she wanted to get to bed. I pulled her jeans down over her slim hips. She was of course not wearing underwear; this was a theme. Her jeans slid off her thighs and I kicked them down to her ankles and growled, "Step out." She did, and I opened her legs and felt her: wet.

I moved my hand to her ass, kicked her legs wider open, and started to spank her.

That, she liked: she could always be warmed up by a little spanking. When her cheeks were red I took off her shirt, and she struggled a little so I grabbed her hair and said, "Wrists against the wall."

She did it, looking nervous and cowed and scared, but as soon as she opened her mouth it was, "Isn't it ironic," from a slutty little bitch who knew what that meant for a change:

Singsong: "Oh, my GOD, you're not going to HURT me, are you?"

"Open," I growled, ball gag already in my hand—I always keep it close when Jill is around.

Her eyes went wide as she was gagged, and that was plenty to get her going even faster than the spanking. She melted into the wall while I drew back my hand and coaxed little muffled yelps out of her with repeated flat-handed blows. Then I started to caress her, feeling her shaved and smooth and wet, and that's when it happened.

I had my eyes on the back of her neck, so I cannot say for sure that she did not sneak her hand down from the wall. That is, of course, what must have happened. She slapped my hand while I felt her up.

Or somebody did.

I opened my mouth to ask if she'd slapped me, but of course she was gagged so I dragged her toward the bed. The writhe and twist of her body told me she was enjoying herself, as did the fact that she was wet when I touched her again. It happened again: I glanced away to suss out the location of my play bag, and SMACK! her hand came down and slapped mine. My eyes were on her hand quickly; it really, really didn't look like it had moved.

"Did you just slap my hand?" I asked her—my undoing, my foolish, foolish undoing.

She looked at me helplessly, as if to say: "Dude...I'm ball-gagged. How exactly would you like me to answer you?"

"Forget it," I said.

I got her on her hands and knees and tucked pillows under her belly to secure her facedown, ass-up. I had leather restraints and a bondage belt in my play bag. I secured her wrists at her sides, cuffed her ankles, and ran ropes to the bedposts to hold her legs open.

The naked girl wriggled and writhed. Goddamn, she looked amazing; I seized my camera and took several pictures, which did more to excite her than even the spanking had done: Jill was very much an exhibitionist.

I went to caress her and found my hand stilled: No. Now that I had her restrained, I did not need to find out if my own hand would get slapped away. That was silly; just fuck the girl, buddy, just fuck this girl silly.

So I did, shedding my clothes and mounting the bed; I slid into her and listened to her crying out behind the ball gag. She shuddered all over as I drove deep into her. I ran my fingernails down her back and she shivered and arched and came. Even with a ball gag in she was a screamer. Like I said, Jill was an exhibitionist; tied to the bed in a cheap motel, knowing truckers and whores might be listening, she could yowl her way through a ball gag until the whole goddamned county knew she was having a freakin' orgasm. Only the singsongy sarcasm was silenced.

Sort of. When we finished, I untied her but left her cuffs on for esthetic value. We cuddled on the bed in the dark and heat and the scent of our bodies. I caressed her back and she languidly kissed my chest.

She spoke softly, back to deadpan:

"I loved it when you were fucking me, how you pinched my nipples. I love it when you pinch them hard like that."

I didn't dare say a word: To show weakness would be to show my throat, like a dog in a fight surrendering to an infinitely more sarcastic dog.

"And, oh, when I was just about to come? How you worked my clit with your hand like that. Mmmmmm…and your thumb in my ass. God, that was good."

"You liked that, did you?" It was my turn to be deadpan, more-deadpan-than-thou, unwilling to surrender even an inch of spectral ground to the ghosts of the Wildflower, however much my heart was, suddenly and inexplicably, racing.

She made a cooing sound. There was no singsong; she was earnest in a way I had never heard her be. "I loved it when you held my hair while you fucked me."

I snapped: "Yeah, okay, I get it."

Jill let out a wicked witchy cackle, tossed her hair like a cat circling to find its place to sleep. She put her head down on my chest, sighed softly, and went to sleep.

She was, of course, fucking with me. I had done none of these things: there had been no reach around; I had not stimulated her ass; I had not pinched Jill's nipples.

The answer was obvious: why else would she have sounded earnest?

She was fucking with me. Or maybe not. The office was closed when we left in the morning, and I've never gotten a hit on the place's real name on the Web, so if it's supposed to be haunted, nobody told the Internet. That vast playground of lunatics and charlatans pretty much harbored every ghost that ever lived, so you'd sort of have to find it there, wouldn't you?

"Jill," when I ask—I still see her occasionally—gets this innocent look on her face, and goes perky and bright-eyed and speaks with an earnestness I never see from her otherwise— neither deadpan nor sarcastic, she seems possessed by some woman other than Jill—a woman who would never fuck with a guy just to see him squirm.

Her smile, too, is innocent. You can practically see the fucking dimples.

"Why, whatever do you mean?" she says, and I always change the subject.

In pace requiescat, ghosts of the Wildflower. You know, she's not actually in the French Foreign Legion, either.

STICKLER FOR DETAILS

Alison Tyler

Monica made the initial connection. "You'll like Master Patrick," she assured me. And then she looked off into space for a moment before editing herself. "Well, *like* might not be the right word. I think you'll appreciate him."

"Appreciate in what way?"

Again, there was that momentary pause, a space between words that I should have tried harder to understand. I'm a journalist, after all. I consider deciphering people's silences almost as important as paying attention to their actual words. But I was doing my best simply to stay focused on the glint of her gray-green eyes after downing two martinis. Monica can drink me under the table.

"He's as much of a stickler for details as you are."

And that's all she would say.

Stickler for details. That phrase resonated within me. I knew what she meant. Whenever I'm working on a fresh project, I spend hours researching. You can find me at the library or online, if facts are the focus point. But when I'm writing public interest pieces, I become a bit of a chameleon. We'd been friends since meeting at the UC Berkeley School of Journalism. Over the years, Monica had seen me blend into a wide variety of organizations, each time I went after a big story.

She'd gone after editorship, landing a spot at a glossy sex magazine. I continued to focus on writing, doing my best to tackle subjects I knew nothing about. When she asked me to write a piece for her on BDSM, she knew that while I talked a good game on paper, in reality, I was a novice. Not only at writing but at living the life. So she decided she'd hook me up with her favorite master. For research purposes only, you understand.

We began with an email dialogue.

> Dear Master Patrick, Monica Blue suggested I write to you for advice on a new article I'm researching. I'm hoping you'll be open to some of my questions.
>   Sincerely,
>   Alison Tyler

The answer was immediate and severe: *Mind your Ps and Qs.*

"What the fuck does that mean?" I asked Monica. I'd read her my letter and the response. Then at her request, I forwarded the actual email to her address. She pulled up the email while talking to me on the phone, and she choked back a laugh as she explained the problem.

"You tried to Top him."

"I did not!"

"Come on. Why didn't you lowercase your I's?"

"My what?"

"Your I's. In your letter, you used capital I's."

"Of course, I did. I'm not insane."

"But he's a Top, and you're, well, not."

"How does he know what I am?"

There was that chuckle again, softly teasing, and I felt my cheeks go pink. Monica had never asked outright about my sexual preferences, but apparently she'd correctly assessed my submissive streak.

"Try again. Use your head."

I felt my teeth clench as I retyped my request. I've been typing at a speed of more than one hundred words a minute since I was eleven. Typing lowercase *I*'s instead of the correct capitals went against everything I'd ever done. It took me minutes rather than seconds to type the incorrect punctuation. "Mind my *P*s and *Q*s my ass," I hissed, as I reread the email:

> Dear Master Patrick, Monica Blue suggested i write to you for advice on a new article i'm researching. i'm hoping you'll be open to some of my questions.
> Sincerely,
> Alison Tyler

But then I looked at the letter again. Was I supposed to sub my name? Lowercase the *A* and the *T*? Was I supposed to cap the *Y* of the *you*s? With a shudder, I deleted the *Sincerely* and simply wrote: *Humbly Yours.*

The answer this time was much more satisfactory, although not much more wordy.

Send me your questions.

So I shot off the list:

How did You become a Master?

How many slaves do You have relationships with at a given time?

What is Your preference, if any, for males or females?

I made sure that anytime I referenced myself I did so in the subservient, lowercase *I* manner, but I have to admit, that little tic wasn't growing on me in any way. I joked to my roommate about having to retype every sentence repeatedly in order to incorrectly punctuate as per Master Patrick's instructions. My fingers rebelled. Not hitting the shift key when I ought to was brutal. Equally disturbing was having to hit the shift to cap the *H*s for *Him* and *His*, because when I referred to Master Patrick, he expected me to cap the *H*s, as if He'd become my God. But when I referred to myself, i was little lowercase me, humble to the nth degree.

Yet I was getting what I wanted from him. Or, rather: *i* was getting what *i* wanted from Him. I just didn't really know that yet.

Our next few emails were professional and courteous. We moved from exchanging emails to meeting in a chatroom, a private area in cyberspace where only He and i could visit. Here, I had to work harder than ever. I couldn't type at my normal speed. Each response required careful thought. A stickler for details, he was. Monica had that right. If I fucked up, if I capped my *I*'s, if I forgot to show him his proper respect, he would end the chat.

Slowly, I came up to speed. Slowly, I felt the cyber room fill in around us. I could see the art on the walls. I could imagine what Master Patrick looked like based on his descriptions: His silver hair, His lean physique. My pussy responded to the bell sound on my computer that would let me know Master Patrick was online, that he was ready for me.

Finally, he suggested we talk in person. He felt that we'd come to a point in our relationship where a face-to-face meeting would help me for my research. This is what I'd been hoping for from the start. I like to see the people I'm writing about. I am a good read at those silent gestures everyone does. The lip licks, earlobe tugs, embarrassed squints, flirty hair tosses that most people don't even realize are part of their daily routine.

But suddenly I was worried.

How in the hell was I going to lowercase my *I*'s if we were face-to-face?

"It's not the punctuation," Monica assured me. "It's the tone in your voice. Your gestures. You'll be lowering your eyes rather than lowercasing your *I*'s."

"I don't know," I said, frightened. I'd never been this nervous about meeting an interview subject before.

"Chalk it up to research," she insisted.

What I didn't admit to Monica, what I could barely admit to myself, was that the exchanges with Master Patrick had turned me on fiercely. And while I might bitch to my roommate about the tedium of retyping each email, I found myself embracing the concept each time I hit SEND.

Dressing for our meeting took me days rather than hours. The care I put into my outfit went beyond anything I'd ever done in the past. Even for graduation, I didn't go this far. After trying and discarding nearly every item in my wardrobe, I settled on a black skirt, silk top, lace-up black boots, and fishnets. As an afterthought, I put a velvet collar around my throat.

I looked at myself carefully in the full-length mirror on the back of my bathroom door. I edited the outfit with as much care as I had any article I'd ever turned in. I wanted to look perfect: no bent corners, no smudged ink. In a way, I was following his directions: minding my *P*s and *Q*s.

The idea of walking into the restaurant and feeling his eyes on me, judging, made me get to our prearranged spot a half hour early.

He beat me anyway.

I mean that in both senses of the word.

He was there, waiting, his silver hair brushed back from his forehead, his suit jacket open over a stark white shirt—no tie, no frills, crisp and smart as Courier font. From his gaze, I realized that I no longer had to worry about my *I*'s *or* my eyes, because the sense of submissiveness fell over me like a cloak. I didn't have to think about how to behave. My body reacted on autopilot. His expression was quiet, serious, and I felt an immediate sense of need. I wanted to be his with a capital *H*. If I had to lowercase my *I*'s forever, I would. If he'd had me lick his boots in this high-end Beverly Hills restaurant, I would have done so without a thought. When I pulled up a chair at the table, when I said my greetings, when I brought out my notebook—every gesture about me whispered of my desires. Every story I'd ever written had led me to this point.

Yet not a single one had prepared me for what came next.

"Put away the book," he said.

I put away my notebook.

"Take off the collar."

Collar.

"You don't wear a collar again unless I put one on you. Do you understand?"

I nodded. He waited until I undid the velvet band around my neck with trembling fingers and handed the scrap of black ribbon over to him.

"Go out to the parking lot."

I stood. I didn't care that the maitre d' was giving me a strange look. I didn't care that I'd just arrived. I didn't even care that I had no idea what he was going to do to me next. I simply walked out to the parking lot.

He came up behind me and gripped my arm, not my hand.

Then he led me to the car, a black sedan, shiny, vintage. He opened the back door, pushed me inside. I sat. I waited. And I realized I didn't care what happened next. I didn't need to know. Had I craved research all my life, the preparing and studying in order to get the facts right?

The only fact that mattered right now was that I did what this man wanted, which was simple. He sat at my side, pulled me over his lap, dragged my black Club Monaco skirt to my hips. He stroked my ass through my black satin panties, slid them down my thighs, let me revel in the feeling of being undressed by a stranger.

And then he started to spank me, hard and fast.

The pain surprised me. I'd written about pain before in a story for Monica's magazine, written about the pleasure that comes right on top of pain. But I'd never felt that sensation for myself. Now, I did. But the feelings were different from anything I'd imagined. How? His hand hurt. The smacks of his palm on my skin made me jump, and a part of my brain cried out to make the pain stop. *Why are you doing this? Why are you letting a stranger spank you?* And another part of my brain silenced that first part, with a *Shhhh. This is what you want. This is what you need, what you've always needed. This is exactly what you always thought it would be like.*

Or was it Patrick speaking? So soft, his voice had tiptoed into my brain.

"This is what you need, isn't it?"

"Yes."

"This is what you wanted when you sent me that simpering little note."

"Yes."

"With your belligerent tone."

Teeth gritted, because I hadn't been belligerent, had I? I'd simply capitalized my fucking *I*'s, like any normal sane person would do. I started to push up, but he thrust me back down, spanking me harder, pushing my thighs apart, spanking my pussy, so that now the pain truly melted into pleasure. Now there was nothing in me that wanted to fight. My hips raised up for him. My legs spread wider. *Spank me harder*, that voice in my brain cried out. *Make it hurt so that i can come,* that lowercase *I* begged. And I realized that the lowercase *I* had always been there. Somewhere. Hidden.

"This is exactly what you need," he said once more, spanking with four fingers against my clit, over and over, so that I came, as hard and as fast as he was spanking me. I couldn't remember ever coming like that before, couldn't remember ever being even half as turned on as I was.

"You want me to spank you whenever you've been bad, don't you?"

"Oh, yes." I was whimpering, mewing. The spanking was what I'd always wanted, and always hoped, and my pussy was a sea of wetness.

"Yes, Sir," I said, through tears, "i want to be Yours." And he petted me and called me his good girl. When I sat up, I saw that his lips were twisted in a little half smile. He'd heard the lowercase *I* in my voice. i had become His in a heartbeat, in a keystroke—in a shift.

TEARS OF ALL KINDS

Tess Danesi

When I walk into the room, it's hard not to notice that something is off. Moments later my brain registers that the table, intended to be used as a desk, is pushed away from the wall and completely bare. The lamp that once rested upon it now sits on the floor in the corner. The chairs beneath the window are crowded together; the desk chair now fills any empty space.

I'm in the bathroom when he enters. I hear him moving about but I don't rush. I need these few moments alone to compose myself for what I know is coming. In the car, his voice low, smooth, chilled, and as serious as death, he said, "I'm going to hurt you, Tess." It's the way he says my name, letting it linger on his tongue, emphasizing and enunciating each consonant, making them reverberate with sadism, that frightens me more than usual. So I brush my teeth; I swig, swirl, and spit mouthwash; I change into my sheer black chemise and I take a few deep breaths before sitting on the bed across from him. Victor leans in and kisses me. His lips, so soft and plush, linger on mine. His tongue pushes past my parted lips and snakes around mine. In that moment, I feel as though I could kiss him forever.

Out of nowhere his palm flies toward my face, I flinch, and part of the blow is deflected to my ear, making it ring. It scares me but I have no time to think before he slaps me again, and my face blooms red with heat and anger and fear eddying around a core of intense arousal.

"Did he come in your face, slut? Did he, you bitch?"

"Yyyyes," I mumble, and he hits me again making me obscenely wet. The room closes in around me; nothing exists but our two bodies, our eyes boring into each other's, trying to read the other's thoughts. His eyes are so cold it makes him seem unflappable and tenacious, immovable in fulfilling his desires of the moment. And what he desires most is my pain.

"Get the rope, Tess," he says. His eyes darken and glisten as the words leave his lips.

I shake my head. "No," I say simply. But it's disingenuous and he knows it.

His voice is soft and liquid, silky. "You haven't come all this way for me to kiss you. Be a good girl, get the rope."

I rise and cross the short distance to my bag, painfully aware of his eyes on me and of that table so oddly barren, but I rummage through it until I have the three skeins of luxurious, decadent black hemp given to me by my dear friend, R, straight from Seattle and Twisted Monk. My friend enjoys thinking of me suffering, lovely girl. Victor doesn't waste time. He starts wrapping rope around my wrists and then thinks he might have to cut the thirty-foot length in two until he notices the careful hand-whipped ends and decides it would be criminal to do so; he'll work with it the way it is. I watch his face, his expression so intent, fully concentrated on the task at hand. He tests his work, slipping a finger between the ropes and my skin, before making me get up and walk to the table.

Thoughts of altars and sacrifice fill my head and soak my sex as I press my chest and belly flat against the hard surface of the table. Victor ties my wrists to the legs of the table, pulling tightly, giving me nearly no slack. Then he walks behind me, forces my legs as far apart as the rope between them will go and secures them equally tightly. He doesn't get the gag yet, not yet, first he has something to show me and I know he wants to hear me whimper. He won't be disappointed.

When he walks away, I try to look back but don't have enough range of motion to be able to see him. I feel like I might burst into tears. My day has been filled with stress, both standard and unexpected, and I am truly terrified at what I imagine he's doing. I don't have long to wonder before he lets me see exactly what has been occupying him: his razor. He places new blades, still wrapped in their protective, waxy paper, on the table in front of me and unfolds his razor.

"Do you know hot sharp these are, bitch? Do you know how still you'd better be when I press the blade against your tit?" he asks while setting the blades into the handle. His eyes have grown cold, so cold, and his manner normally so warm and cheery is equally icy. I know nothing save my safeword will divert him from what he has in mind. If it will at all; no matter how many times we are together, how many times he has shown concern for me, I am never quite certain I can stop him. And restrained like this, oh, god, I don't have a chance. And yet, though no amount of tears, no begging, no screaming, nothing except one little word that I am loath to utter will divert him from his goal, my heartbeat races, my palms dampen, and my wetness leaves no doubt that I am insanely (yes, insanely is perfect) aroused.

He leans in, his face inches from mine, regarding me, feasting on the fear in my eyes, on the tremor in my lower lip. Devouring these signs, he gorges on the physical manifestations of my terror, a terror mixed with a degree of trust large enough for me to allow this, even to crave it.

"You have such a pretty face, Tess," he says as he brings something to my cheek. I don't know what—his finger, the handle of the razor, the blade. Seeing him near my face with the blade has made me squeeze my eyes closed in terror. I just can't bear to look. My mouth is so dry; I don't think I can answer when he speaks to me. "You'd best stay very still, don't you think, baby?"

Despite my closed eyes, I manage to cry, though it's not the immense flood I expected and I know would have been drowning me now had I not had a pomegranate martini with dinner. I had been close to tears waiting for him to pick me up at the station due to my day, a series of aggravating occurrences and stressors that now culminate with me at his mercy. But now, while not even buzzed from the alcohol, I am calmer. I'm not sure if that's a good thing. My tears, the few times he has been able to make me weep uncontrollably, are intoxicating to him and cathartic to me. He moves the razor as I mumble over and over, "Not my face, baby. Oh, god, please, not my face." I don't think he'd cut me, I really don't, and not my face, but I don't know, not for sure, no, not for sure.

He steps back, and through tear-clouded eyes I see his cock, so hard that it's straining at the pants he has yet to remove. I lick my dry lips at the thought of taking him in my mouth.

"You're not getting my cock yet, bitch," he spits out. His accompanying cruel derisive laugh makes me wish I wasn't tied up so I could slap him.

Behind me again, he bends down, gently kisses my neck,

my shoulders, my arm before licking my earlobe, making me tremble even more; I sense exactly what this is—the calm before the storm. Whispering into my ear, rubbing the silky fabric of my lingerie between his fingers, he says, "You didn't want to wear this again, now did you?"

I mumble my one-word answer, "No."

The sound of the razor catching on the sheer stretchy fabric is brief as it rapidly slices down the center right above my spine. I shiver thinking about all the delicate mechanisms under my skin: muscles, sinews, disks, bones; the very things that allow me to walk. My thoughts are disrupted as the razor reaches the top of my panties and splits them apart easily, the blade so damn close to my ridiculously soaked sex. He takes his time with me, enjoying each shudder, each quiver, the way I bite my lower lip, the way my eyes go wide with fear as he traces lines in my skin with the razor. I don't know if he's cut me. I don't think so. But I feel an unmistakable sharpness that can only be the blade. My face is damp with sweat and tears. I think I'm begging him to stop, not to cut me, please, please, please. I don't know what I'm thinking as the razor trails over the rounded globes of my ass and down my thighs. My emotions, my fears, my lust are all jumbled together in a Gordian knot that defies undoing.

Then he places the razor on the table and walks to the bed to retrieve his belt.

He only has the belt he uses for work, having forgotten his preferred one at home. This one is of stiff leather tipped with a shiny silver buckle. The left side of my face is pressed to the table so I can see as much of the room as possible; it's an effort to retain whatever vestige of control I imagine I have. I see him wind the belt around his hand until he has the desired length, and my body stiffens in anticipation. Before he can strike me, I ask him to get the gag from my bag. I'm afraid of screaming too loudly in this family- and business-type hotel. He complies gladly with my request.

I begin to panic when he closes the strap around the back of my head. I don't mind having the gag in my mouth but the thought of not being able to remove it when I need to is enough to push me toward the brink of hysteria. I swallow back my apprehension, willing myself to be calm, recalling that the straps of this gag never stay in place, and I will easily be able to divest myself of it should I need to. Victor is used to my semisubmission. In fact, he relishes my struggle, both physically with him and internally in my own head. When he ultimately triumphs, it's a much greater victory.

My time for contemplation is short lived. Suddenly, the air moves, parting as the belt slices through it before landing on my ass with a resounding crack. I don't scream, I breathe and think it will be fine, I will be fine, I can handle this. But each ensuing strike increases in violence. I feel the rope tightening around my wrists, digging in as I struggle uselessly. There is no way I am getting free of this until he wants me free. He's tied me so securely that I am forced up onto my toes and my calves vibrate with exertion. The straps of the gag slide down my hair, and I am able to pop the gag out enough to shout my dismay when the belt lands on an area already bruised and sore from his repeated torment. I scream again and he still hits me over and over. The sharp crack of the belt accompanies each whack. I try to contain my resistance, my screams. I tell myself to stay still, to stop struggling, but it's as if I can't control the flow that bubbles up from some well deep inside me. My ass glows fiery crimson as he methodically, sadistically abuses me. He stops and I am suddenly aware of his breathing; it has become as heavy and jagged as mine. His face drips with sweat. The room seems deadly quiet despite the fact that he's turned on the television to cover the thunder-crack of the belt and my ensuing shrieks.

My eyes close as I finally stop struggling and try to regain some composure. He doesn't allow me long. He pulls my head back by my hair, so taut that each strand pulsates with the beat of my heart, and with the other hand he spreads my cheeks apart. His clothes have been shed, and his cock presses against the tight bud of my ass.

"No, no, fuck, no, Victor," I scream, tensing and making the inevitable lubeless thrust that much more painful. The belt was nothing compared to this; this is brutal, excruciating. I don't think I can bear it, and I feel my safeword on my tongue, but hesitate for a moment. In that moment, he pushes even harder, entering me. But it's too much and I wail in agony before I say the one word that stops him cold.

"I can't, I can't, I can't. I'm sorry, so sorry, baby," I find myself muttering stupidly. I needn't be sorry and I know it, but in that moment I wanted to give him what he wanted and so I find myself ridiculously repentant.

He pulls on a condom and thrusts into me, this time sliding smoothly past my slick, engorged folds while pushing my face into the table. I don't even realize I'm screaming; this time my screams are of debauched pleasure. This time I want it rough, as rough as he can give it. This time I want his cock penetrating me to my core. This time I want him to keep fucking me relentlessly. I find my entire body quivering, starting with the clenching of the muscles in my cunt, as his cock hits my G-spot again and again. He stops too soon.

"Baby..." I whimper.

"Shut up, bitch," he says. His eyes are still flat and dark as he climbs on the table and looms above me with his cock, hard as steel and purple with blood, in his hand. He ejaculates so strongly that the first stream is propelled high, missing me entirely. The second falls all over my back and ass. It feels warm in the chill of the air-conditioning. He jumps down and walks away, leaving me tied there trying to catch my breath. His seed has landed on me in individual droplets reminiscent of warm, salty tears. I feel each drop begin to trickle down my ass, flowing along my thighs. My mind tells me it's my body weeping. Somehow, though I can't cry the way I want to, his come has transformed into my tears, tears that continue to stream over the taut satin skin of my ass and down my tense, quaking legs.

He comes back from the bathroom and clicks open his knife, forcing the point of it under my chin, stilling me again. He watches my eyes open wider as I begin to tremble. He smiles, a dark, cold smile, a smile filled with glee at the way I cringe and how my breathing catches raggedly. The cold, hard blade makes its way down my neck, along my side and up my back. He prods me with the point until I beg him to stop. I think I'm still begging when we hear knocking at the door.

"Oh, fuck," I say.

"Shh," he says, taking control of the situation in a way that somewhat eases my mind. He shouts at the unwelcome presence to wait a moment before going to the door. Still bound, I hear him open the door a crack and speak to someone. He walks back to me. "It's hotel security."

"Nooo," I interrupt him. "You're kidding me."

"No, baby, it is. He wants to speak to you. Make sure you're all right."

"Fuck, fuck, fuck. Perhaps you'd better untie me then," I say, even as he has begun unwinding the ropes from the legs of the table. Trailing rope that I manage to discard from my wrists but not my ankles before reaching the door, I open it a crack, trying to keep my nakedness hidden from view.

The man is gray haired and stern faced. "Are you all right,

ma'am?" he asks, scanning my face for signs of distress.

"I'm fine, really, I'm fine," I mutter. I can feel the smile on my face, one there not to convince him of my safety but simply because like always, after the intensity of what preceded, I am ecstatic. All the stress has been drained from my body, and I feel so light that I think I could float.

"All right then," he says, "just tone down the screaming please."

After a cross-my-heart-and-hope-to-die assurance that we will keep it down, Victor and I walk back to the bed and fall laughing in each other's arms. I catch a glimpse of myself in the mirror; hair wild, eyes and skin glowing brightly. It's a look of feral radiance, one I wish I could muster every day.

Victor ponders whether this particular chain of hotels will be blacklisting him in the future.

"We need to find the local equivalent of that hot-sheets, red-room motel I like so much. No one cares what goes on in there," I say. "Plus I like hearing the sounds of other couples fucking."

"You are such a whore, Tess," he says with a smile full of warmth, amiability, and humor. The beast has been momentarily sated but I know, as does he, that it's only temporary and that by morning the low rumble of the beast will be reverberating in my ear as he wraps a fistful of my hair around his hand and once again impales my greedy, yielding cunt with his perfect cock.

ONCE MORE BENEATH THE EXIT SIGN

Stephen Elliott

On the fourth day together we broke up. We had planned this for a while; not the breakup, but the four days. Her husband wanted to spend a week with her over Christmas in Chicago, get her out of the Bay Area, and so she wanted to spend four days with me when they returned. That was the deal they worked out.

We had been dating for over five months and her marriage was falling apart. Eden was in one of those open marriages, the kind where you see other people, the kind everybody says doesn't work. Except her husband didn't see other people, which was fine because they had different desires but then I came along and we fell in love and in the nine years she'd been with her husband she had never fallen in love with someone else. Her husband told her he felt ripped off. She told me he hated me but I didn't think it was my responsibility. It was the situation that was killing him. I was incidental. Anyway, I had my own problems.

We spent almost the entire four days in bed and when we

broke up there were condoms on the floor, latex gloves covered in lube, a rattan cane flecked with blood. There was rope spread under the desk and near the closet and attached to the bed frame. There was a roller box full of clamps and clothespins and collars and wrist cuffs and a gas mask and leather hood pulled from under the bed so we had to step over it when we got up to go to the bathroom. There was a strap-on dildo and holster sitting on top of a box of photographs next to the door, a purple silicone butt plug near the radiator.

Love is a hard thing to explain. I didn't mean to fall in love with a married woman. I had successfully not fallen in love so many times that when Eden told me she was married I didn't even flinch. We were in a cafe and she was wearing all black. It was the first time we met. She mentioned her husband, said he was away for a couple of days. "I tell him everything," she said. "I told him we were meeting for coffee." She wanted to be sure I understood that he was her primary, that I could never be first in her life.

Two and a half weeks later I was sitting on her kitchen floor while she prepared dinner—slicing eggplants, soaking them in salt and transferring them to the stove. The flames licked the bottom of the pot and I was careful not to move. I didn't want to get in the way. She leaned down and took my face in her hands.

"Look at me," she said. "I love you."

"I love you too," I replied.

The breakup didn't come from nowhere. I had lost my mind in the week she was in Chicago. I called friends I hadn't seen in years just so I could tell them my story: that I was in love with a married woman and I slept with her once a week and the other six nights I slept alone. My thoughts were consumed with her and I couldn't do my work. My savings were nearly depleted. I lost my adjunct position at the university when I failed to show up for two classes. I saw her two other days each week during the day while her husband was at work and on days we spent apart we spoke for an hour on the phone. Sometimes I saw her on the weekend as well and we went dancing and she came back to my house to sleep over an extra time. I told my friends I saw her more than her husband did, as if that counted for something.

They said, "Get rid of her."

I said, "What if it's me? What if I'm not capable of love?" And what I meant was that I was thirty-four years old and I had never been in a serious relationship in my entire life. I had never been in love. I had minimal contact with my family. There was no one in the world who depended on me in any way.

Before we broke up she told me the story of meeting her husband. They had been neighbors in the Haight District. It's the neighborhood that had been the capital of free love and counterculture forty years ago before succumbing to drug addiction and excess and is now populated with fashion boutiques and street hustlers, junkies sticking themselves against the frosted windows and smearing their open sores on the parking meter in front of a bar shaped like a spaceship, the worst of the rich and poor.

She had a boyfriend and lived with him downstairs and her would-be husband lived upstairs with his wife. They rarely spoke, instead she spoke with the wife and he spoke with the boyfriend. But years later he was divorced from his wife and Eden was no longer with her boyfriend and he called and asked would she like to go see a band. He'd fathered a child since the last time they met.

He didn't try anything that first date, because he's a gentleman, with his short dark hair and innocent face. He's tall and thin, straight shouldered and from a good family with a good name. He works in a brokerage, wears a suit to work and a black leather jacket. He asked her on a second date and then asked what her deal was. She explained that she was seeing someone, this guy. But the guy had moved to Seattle. So now they were still together but she was seeing other people as well. She said she liked seeing other people. She didn't believe in only seeing one person anymore, in constraining her love, not fulfilling her desires. She was never going to be monogamous again; she had tried and it made her unhappy. This was Northern California, a woman's body was her own and people didn't have to abide by the old rules if they didn't want to. He asked if he could be one of those other people she was seeing and she said yes and six months later they were living together and then they were married and she became a mother to his son.

We had almost broken up on our first of four days. I had arrived to pick her up at her house badly damaged and trying to hide it. Why was I so sad? I thought it was the holidays. Christmas is my least favorite day of the year. And my girlfriend had been gone, unreachable, away with her husband. And we'd had a fight before she left. And my friends were also out of town. But maybe I'm just a sad person. I make decisions assuming that I'm probably going to kill myself anyway. It's just a matter of time. That's my big secret.

Christmas was over; it was cold and the streets were wet. It was eight in the morning and I was on time but not early because her husband left for work at seven thirty and he and I had already run into each other too many times. They owned a house in Berkeley, a small ranch house built in the backyard of a larger house. Their bedroom was different from mine, dominated by a king-size bed with a short space between two large dressers. Her husband's laundry sat in a small pile in the corner and I waited there while Eden showered.

She had been miserable in Chicago where the streets were so cold and her feet hurt from walking the city. She said they'd been to the library and the museum, the Art Institute, and Clark and Division. They'd taken a train to Addison and seen Wrigley Field. I was from Chicago and I held my tongue because I thought they had missed everything.

Later that day, in my room which is just a yellow space I rent in someone else's apartment and is filled with everything I own in the whole world because I own so little, before the box full of sex toys was all the way out from under the bed and maybe there were just one or two gloves on the floor, she told me she didn't think it could work. And we broke up. But then she changed her mind. In the morning she broke up with me again, and again changed her mind. We never left the bed.

I told a joke about Arabs sending threatening email in order to get the federal government to come out and dig up their yard for them.

On the third day we didn't break up. She caned me, then tied me spread-eagle to the bed and got on top of me. "Don't come," she said. And then we lay in bed talking about how much we loved each other and the various things we had done together. It was a list that included Nashville and honky-tonk bars and packed lunch on cliffs overlooking the San Francisco Bay. We'd been to readings and parades and movies and shopped for organic produce at an Asian grocery in Berkeley. We always held hands. We'd been dancing and we danced together well. We spent hours on the phone agreeing on the political issues of the day. Beneath it was this: we were sexually compatible. She liked to hurt people and I liked to be hurt. She liked it when I cried and I wanted to cry all the time.

She turned me over and tied my arms forward and my legs spread and a rope around my ankles and thighs to keep my knees bent and greased her strap-on and slid it inside of me and fucked me violently. "I'm not going to go easy," she said. "I want to hear you."

When we were done she said, "I did all the things you like today."

"You did," I told her. She asked me why I thought she did these things and I said because she loved me and I told her I loved her too.

We went out that night, the only time in four days we left the bed. But not for long. We went to a noodle house with small round tables and I looked at other couples on dates or just eating dinner. Everyone was in pairs; no one was eating alone. There were couples who had just met, trying to impress each other, still a long way from that moment of truth, still hiding their core, afraid of what the other might think when he or she saw them whole. Older couples were there, people who had been together many years and stopped talking altogether. Each person in each couple was unique with his or her special needs. I wondered what those needs were and if they were being met. In her book *Psychoanalysis: The Impossible Profession,* Janet Malcolm tells how a famous analyst was once asked, "What would you call an interpersonal relationship where infantile wishes, and defenses against those wishes, get expressed in such a way that the persons within that relationship don't see each other for what they objectively are but, rather, view each other in terms of their infantile needs and their infantile conflicts? What would you call that?" He replied, "I'd call that life."

From the noodle house we went to a bar. There were people I knew at the bar and they were playing darts. One of them was moving to France. "I'll be gone six months," he told me. He was going to finish a novel he'd been working on for years. I didn't want to know about it. I thought the bar was cold and empty and there was too much open space.

Then on the fourth day we broke up for real.

It was 1:40 in the afternoon and the curtains were open. We could see my neighbor sitting at a computer in a square of light on the fourth floor of the large apartment building across the street. She asked if I remembered when we first got together and she told me how she was territorial and jealous and I had said I could be monogamous to her. She told me she was consumed with jealousy. It wasn't a matter of me seeing other women, she was burning with the idea that I might desire them, which I didn't deny. She had never felt this kind of jealousy before.

I told her I didn't know what I wanted because I had never been in a relationship like this. I didn't know what it would do to me. I didn't tell her that I was in free fall. I didn't say what I thought, which was that this was about other things, that we both wanted our lives back and we had run our course together and there was nowhere left to go. I wanted to write and she wanted to save her marriage and I wanted to find someone who would love me all the time even though I doubted I would. Even though I knew deep inside that being with her part time and sharing her was more than I would ever get full time with someone else. But we had stopped growing. Everything had stopped. We were stuck and there was nowhere for us to go and there was no acceptable change. She wasn't going to leave her husband and the depression that lifted when we met had returned and engulfed me and was getting worse.

Our four days was two hours and twenty minutes from ending. She was meeting her husband at Union Square. They

were going to go shopping, and then maybe see a movie. It was
New Year's Eve tomorrow and she wanted to get groceries so on
New Year's Day she could have a traditional breakfast with fish
and rice, and friends invited over to start the new year correctly.
Earlier in our relationship she mentioned that she hoped we
could get to where I could come over for New Year's and be
comfortable with her husband and he with me. But we never got
to that point. I never fully joined her harem with her husband
who has stayed true to his wife these nine years while she went
through a parade of men looking to see if it was possible to love
two men at the same time and finally deciding on me. Maybe
it was the sex. We fucked like animals. She rarely had sex with
her husband. He wasn't into the kinky things we were into. He
hadn't grown up eroticizing his childhood trauma the way I had.
And he had married a sadist.

We had two hours and twenty minutes and she said she
couldn't do it and I agreed. Then I waited a heartbeat and I
said, "So we're breaking up?" And this time I knew it was true
because I started to cry and she grabbed me closely and I buried
my face inside her hair.

"I can't leave you."

"I don't want to be without you," I said.

"Then don't be."

But five minutes later I asked what was going to happen and
she said we were done and I nodded my head. Still we stayed in
bed and I pressed my lips against hers, placed my hand on her
ass, ran my palm over the contours of her backside to the top of
her legs. I kissed her deeply and cried more.

"Don't cry," she said. I'd cried in front of her so many times
over five months. At first I had been embarrassed but then I
realized she liked it so I cried freely. I was shocked by my own
propensity for tears. I never knew I had so many of them and

they were so close to the surface. I would cry when she was hitting me and she wouldn't even stop. She would beat me the whole way through until the tears were gone and I relaxed again and I came back to her. She said she wanted to provide a space for that little boy inside of me. But now she didn't want me to cry anymore and I tried to put the tears back into wherever they came from and I succeeded and then they came again and then they stopped.

Still I knew I was making my own decision. There were things I could say to keep it going and I wasn't saying them. I was once again jumping from a burning building, abandoning what seemed like an unsustainable situation, something I had been doing since I ran from home when I was thirteen, moving out to the streets of Chicago. I never went back. I never did. I've been running away my entire life.

I reached into that tub next to the bed and grabbed a condom from a paper bag. I fucked her hard and fast and in a way unlike any I had ever fucked her before. She began to scream and then her own tears came, drenching her face until she resembled a mermaid. This was our due. We were breaking up and we were entitled to this sex and we were going to have it. I slammed into her with everything I had. It was like fucking in a storm. I gripped her legs, the flesh of her thighs. I sniffed at her neck. "C'mon," I said, and she screamed and shook with orgasms. Then we rolled over and she was on top of me with her fingers in my hair and one hand on my throat. We were still fucking. She pinched my nipple hard, she reached down between my legs. It didn't matter. I wasn't going to come.

"I want to come," I said.

"Okay," she whispered.

"I can't come inside you."

She got off of me. We were running out of time. I lay next

to her and masturbated quickly and came into the rubber. She pulled the rubber off of me, tying a knot in one swift motion, pulling the end with her thumb and forefinger, striding across the room while I watched the naked triangle of her legs tapering into her ankles.

She tried to call her husband. She didn't want to meet him downtown, she wanted to meet him at home. But he had already left the bank.

"I have to shower," she said.

"He's your husband," I told her. "You don't need to shower for him. He's seen you dirty before."

"I'm not showering for him," she said. "I'm showering for myself."

I followed her into the bathroom. My shower is small, barely room for the two of us. We used the chocolate-scented soap she bought me. She was always buying me fancy soaps. This one was composed of dark brown and white blocks and thin lines and the bar separated into its parts while we were scrubbing.

"I have to go," she said.

"I can't walk you to the train," I told her. "I don't want to break down at the station."

I got dressed while she dressed. I pulled on my jeans and an undershirt and a T-shirt. I laced up my gym shoes.

"Why are you getting dressed if you're not walking me to the train station?" she asked.

"I don't know," I said.

It was raining and I offered her my umbrella. I lose my umbrellas so I never buy expensive ones. The umbrella cost six dollars. I considered giving her my necklace but I knew she wouldn't wear it. She turned down the umbrella. She was going to get wet. We moved toward the door of my room. She was wearing her long blue wool coat.

"Don't go," I said suddenly. I didn't even know where it came from and my hand was in the pocket of her coat and her hand was along my neck and the back of my head. I could have turned into an animal, a dinosaur. I could have grown a giant tail and swung it and broken the windows and the table legs and smashed the bed to pieces.

"Walk me out," she said.

I walked her downstairs, out the front to the entryway to the building. I lit her cigarette on the steps. We kept having one more kiss. She was going to be very late to meet her husband. But he would probably be relieved, his ordeal was over. He would make rules next time, communicate better, draw lines in the sand. There would be no sleepover nights with the next boyfriend. No boys in the house when he came home. But for the foreseeable future he would have to hear about me and comfort his wife while she romanticized our love and cried in his arms.

You concentrate on your time alone, you never think about how hard it is to be in bed with someone else, thinking about you, she said once.

She opened the gate and stepped onto the sidewalk and the rain hit her immediately. It blew horizontally in sharp little beads. I ran down the stairs and grabbed the gate and watched her walk to the corner. I waited for her to turn around. She never looked back. She crossed south and then the light changed and she walked east in front of the housing projects toward the station and the train, which would take her home.

ABOUT THE AUTHORS

By day, **JAX BAYNARD** is a financial investment advisor. By night, she makes her own (and her clients') fantasies come true. This part-time dominatrix's short fiction has appeared online and in several literary journals.

Not very long ago, **TESS DANESI** was your average neurotic wife, mother, and accountant living a life of not-so-quiet desperation in the suburbs of New York City. Tess found her salvation and sanity by exploring D/s and using those explorations as a basis for creating erotic fiction with a D/s twist. She blogs about her varied exploits and often tumultuous life at Urban Gypsy (www.nyc-urban-gypsy.blogspot.com) and somehow finds time to review sex toys. Tess was a winner of Babeland's erotica contest and has been published in *Time Out New York*.

BELLA DEAN is new to the business of dirty stories. She still blushes when she types but has no plans to give up writing. She lives with her small family in her small house in her small town. Her work has appeared in *Afternoon Delight*.

STEPHEN ELLIOTT is the author of the novel *Happy Baby* and the story collection *My Girlfriend Comes to the City and Beats Me Up*. Mr. Elliott is the founding editor of the Rumpus.

A. D. R. FORTE's erotic short fiction appears in several anthologies from Cleis Press, including *Hurts So Good*; *Yes, Ma'am;* and *Girls on Top*. Her stories have also been featured in multiple Black Lace Wicked Words collections and in fantasy erotica from Circlet Press. (And yes, she still likes to travel by bus.) Please visit www.adrforte.com for more information.

SHANNA GERMAIN learned any number of things in her high school art room, euchre and sex being the two she continues to this day. Eventually, she hopes to get really good at both. You can read her work in places like *Best American Erotica*, *Best Bondage Erotica 2*, *Best Gay Bondage Erotica*, *Best Lesbian Erotica*, *Dirty Girls*, *Frenzy*, *Playing with Fire*, and on her website, www.shannagermain.com.

MALCOLM HARRIS wrote stories about his sexual fantasies until they became reality, at which point his Mistress required he keep a journal of his thoughts and experiences. "Mr. Smith, Ms. Jones Will See You Now" is from that time, and his first published work. Mr. Harris lives in Connecticut with his wife and a middle-aged basset hound.

MICHAEL HEMMINGSON's work has appeared recently in *Frenzy* and the *Journal of Sex Research*. The Borgo Press and (the "new") Olympia Press have been reissuing his many out-of-print Blue Moon titles, either under new titles, pen names, or same titles and same name, from *The Stripper* to *Bad Karma and Kinky Sex*.

KRISTINA LLOYD is the author of three erotic novels, *Darker Than Love*, *Asking for Trouble*, and *Split*, all published by Black Lace. Her short stories have appeared in numerous anthologies and magazines, in both the United Kingdom and the United States, and her novels have been translated into German, Dutch, and Japanese. She has a masters distinction in twentieth century literature and has been described as "a fresh literary talent" who "writes sex with a formidable force." She lives in Brighton on the south coast of England. For more, visit kristinalloyd.wordpress.com.

NIKKI MAGENNIS is a Scottish writer and artist whose work has appeared in many anthologies, including *Hurts So Good*, *J Is for Jealousy*, and the *Mammoth Book of Best New Erotica Volumes 7* and *8*. Her second novel, *The New Rakes*, is out now from Virgin Black Lace. Find out more at: nikkimagennis.blogspot.com.

SOMMER MARSDEN's work has appeared in dozens of anthologies. Some of her favorites include *I Is for Indecent*, *J Is for Jealousy*, *L Is for Leather*, *Spank Me*, *Tie Me Up*, *Whip Me*, *Ultimate Lesbian Erotica '08*, *Love at First Sting*, *Open for Business*, *Tasting Her*, *Hurts So Good*, *Seduce Me*, *Best Women's Erotica 2009*, *Seduction*, *Lust at First Bite*, and *Yes, Sir*. She lives in Maryland where she drinks red wine, writes, runs, reads, and eats way too much candy. She's a bit obsessed when it comes to sex, emails, and reality TV. Visit her at SmutGirl.blogspot. com to keep up with her dirty ramblings.

No, **ANNETTE MILLER** isn't her real name, and no, Jim isn't his real name, but she really did get off tied to the seat in a movie theater. You probably don't know her, but you might. "Annette" works as a freelance technical writer and editor and does naughty things on the weekends.

DAKOTA REBEL lives in Detroit, Michigan. She loves the city at night and the shopping during the day. Her favorite things include David Bowie and vampire movies, the Beatles and Alkaline Trio. Dakota is the author of several novels and short stories published with various houses. Visit her at www.dakotarebel.com.

TERESA NOELLE ROBERTS has published several erotic romance novellas with Phaze, and her short erotic fiction has appeared in *Caught Looking: Erotic Tales of Voyeurs and Exhibitionists*, *Best Lesbian Erotica 2009*, *Hurts So Good*, *Spanked: Red-Cheeked Erotica*, *Dirty Girls*, and dozens of other collections with titles that make her mother blush. Teresa is a published poet and also writes erotica with a coauthor as Sophie Mouette. In the spare time she doesn't really have, Teresa is an avid cook, a gardener, a belly dancer, an aspiring yogini, and a member of the Society for Creative Anachronism.

Of late, **THOMAS S. ROCHE** writes weird fiction and erotica, and nonfiction on cryptozoology, ghost hunting, paranormal events, parapsychology, organized crime, science, technology, sexuality, sexual politics, music, and all matters goth. He teaches at San Francisco Sex Information (www.sfsi.org) and blogs at www.thomasroche.com and www.techyum.com. He is currently at work on a memoir, a photo book, and several novels.

DIANA ST. JOHN has been spinning sexy stories since college, even earning an A for the smutty tale she submitted in a college writing class in response to an essay prompt on Michel Foucault's *Discipline and Punish*. She lives in a small town nestled in the foothills of the Sierra Nevadas in Northern California with her family—and her stripper pole—and blogs regularly about sex and spirit at skinprayers.blogspot.com. Her work has appeared in *Hurts So Good*.

BROOKE STERN has published a novel, dozens of stories, and has edited a few anthologies for a variety of publishers, most of which have weathered the economic downturn about as well as hedge funds and interest-only mortgages.

DONNA GEORGE STOREY is the author of *Amorous Woman* (Neon/Orion), a semi-autobiographical tale of an American's steamy love affair with Japan. Her short fiction has been published in more than ninety journals and anthologies, including *The Mile High Club: Plane Sex Stories, Do Not Disturb: Hotel Sex Stories, X: The Erotic Treasury, Best Women's Erotica*, and *Mammoth Book of Best New Erotica*. She currently writes columns for the Erotica Readers and Writers Association: "Cooking up a Storey," about her favorite topics— delicious sex, well-crafted food, and mind-blowing writing and "Shameless Self-Promotion" about book promotion for erotica writers. Read more at www.DonnaGeorgeStorey.com.

SOPHIA VALENTI is an editor, writer, and lifelong New Yorker. She enjoys uncovering sexy secrets, attending sordid soirees, and writing all about them. If she's not reading or writing, she's probably drinking coffee. Her erotica has appeared in *Afternoon Delight* and *Playing with Fire*. Visit her at sophiavalenti.blogspot.com.

XAN WEST is the pseudonym of a New York City BDSM/
sex educator and writer. Xan's work can be found in *Best SM
Erotica Volume 2, Got a Minute?, Love at First Sting, Men on
the Edge, Leathermen, Backdraft, Hurts So Good*, brotherout-
sider.org, *Frenzy, Best Women's Erotica 2008 and 2009*, and
Best Gay Erotica 2009, and the upcoming *DADDIES, SexTime*,
and *Cruising for Bad Boys*. Xan can be reached at Xan_West@
yahoo.com.

RITA WINCHESTER is a domestic goddess who likes to be tied
up in her kitchen (or anywhere else). She is happily committed
to one very sexy partner. Her work has cropped up in places
like Ruthie's Club, the Erotic Woman, For the Girls, *I Is for
Indecent, Mammoth Lesbian Erotica, Tasting Her, Frenzy*, and
Afternoon Delight. You can drop her a line (or a rope) at Rita_
Winchester@yahoo.com.

KRISTINA WRIGHT (www.kristinawright.com) is an author
whose steamy erotica has appeared in more than sixty anthologies, including the Cleis Press collections *Afternoon Delight:
Erotica for Couples* and *Playing with Fire: Taboo Erotica*, as
well as the Black Lace anthologies *Seduction* and *Liaisons* and
Avon Red's *Bedding Down: A Collection of Winter Erotica*.
Kristina's idea of a vacation includes a luxury hotel with a view,
room service, and a bathtub big enough for two. But that's
another story entirely.

ABOUT THE EDITOR

Called a "Trollop with a Laptop" by *East Bay Express*, a "Literary Siren" by *Good Vibrations*, and "Cheeky" by ERWA, **ALISON TYLER** has made being naughty her official trademark. Her sultry short stories have appeared in more than one hundred anthologies including titles edited by Violet Blue, Stephen Elliott, Maxim Jakubowski, Rachel Kramer Bussel, Tristan Taormino, and Zane.

Ms. Tyler is loyal to coffee (black), lipstick (red), and tequila (straight). She has tattoos, but no piercings; a wicked tongue, but a quick smile; and bittersweet memories, but no regrets. She believes it won't rain if she doesn't bring an umbrella, prefers hot and dry to cold and wet, and loves to spout her favorite motto: "You can sleep when you're dead." She chooses Led Zeppelin over the Beatles, the Cure over the Smiths, and the Stones over everyone—yet although she appreciates good rock, she has a pitiful weakness for '80s hair bands.

In all things important, she remains faithful to her partner of nearly fifteen years, but she still can't choose just one perfume.

Find her on the web at www.alisontyler.com, or visit www.myspace.com/alisontyler if you want to be her friend.